D0108774

THE TELL-TALE START

THE MISADVENTURES OF Edgar & Allan Poe

BOOK ONE

THE TELL-TALE START

Gordon McAlpine

illustrations by Sam Zuppardi

VIKING
An Imprint of Penguin Group (USA) Inc.

VIKING
Published by the Penguin Group
Penguin Young Readers Group, 345 Hudson Street, New York, New York 10014, U.S.A.
Penguin Group (Canada), 90 Eglinton Avenue East, Suite 700, Toronto, Ontario, Canada
M4P 2Y3 (a division of Pearson Penguin Canada Inc.)
Penguin Books Ltd, 80 Strand, London WC2R 0RL, England
Penguin Ireland, 25 St Stephen's Green, Dublin 2, Ireland (a division of Penguin Books Ltd)
Penguin Group (Australia), 250 Camberwell Road, Camberwell, Victoria 3124, Australia
(a division of Pearson Australia Group Pty Ltd)
Penguin Books India Pvt Ltd, 11 Community Centre, Panchsheel Park,
New Delhi – 110 017, India
Penguin Group (NZ), 67 Apollo Drive, Rosedale, Auckland 0632, New Zealand
(a division of Pearson New Zealand Ltd.)
Penguin Books (South Africa) (Pty) Ltd, 24 Sturdee Avenue, Rosebank,
Johannesburg 2196, South Africa

Penguin Books Ltd, Registered Offices: 80 Strand, London WC2R 0RL, England

First published in the United States of America by Viking,
a division of Penguin Young Readers Group, 2013

10 9 8 7 6 5 4 3 2 1

Text copyright © Gordon McAlpine, 2013
Illustrations copyright © Sam Zuppardi, 2013
All rights reserved

LIBRARY OF CONGRESS CATALOGING-IN-PUBLICATION DATA IS AVAILABLE
ISBN 978-0-670-78491-2

Printed in the USA
Set in Stempel Schneidler
Book design by Eileen Savage

To my Dad—G. M.

To Jade—S. Z.

A black cat crossing your path signifies
that the animal is going somewhere.

—Groucho Marx

CONTENTS

THE TELL-TALE START

NO ORDINARY SCHOOL DAY

EDGAR and Allan Poe sat beside each other in the back row of their homeroom class, asleep. They'd been up late the night before, reading the latest in their favorite series, True Stories of Horror, and now they leaned shoulder-to-shoulder, head-to-head, together in dreamland. Like little sleeping angels. . . .

Well, maybe not angels.

The Poe twins bore an uncanny resemblance to their famous great-great-great-great granduncle Edgar Allan Poe, the author of gothic tales so horrifying that for close to two centuries they have kept readers awake long into the night. Edgar and Allan were proud of their great-great-great-great granduncle and happy to look like him. Nonetheless, the resemblance ensured they would never be mistaken for run-of-the-mill boys.

The author Edgar Allan Poe as he looked in the 1840s

The Poe twins today

Edgar   *Allan*

It wasn't just external similarities that the boys shared with their great-great-great-great granduncle—they also shared his taste for the thrilling and unexpected.

Intrigue, coded messages, dark secrets . . .

And in at least one way, the boys' minds were even

more unusual than their famous uncle's. If at this moment you could observe the insides of their sleepy heads rather than just the outsides, you'd discover the following:

Edgar was dreaming he was Allan.

Allan was dreaming he was Edgar.

The boys were jolted awake when their homeroom teacher, Mrs. Rosecrans, slammed her stapler on her desk (inadvertently squashing an unlucky ant that happened to be making its way toward the glazed doughnut Mrs. Rosecrans had set beside her attendance book). Now Edgar was no longer sure he was not actually Allan, as he had been in the dream, and Allan was not sure that he was not actually Edgar. They looked at each other and saw only their own faces looking back. It happened to them all the time.

No big deal.

No one could tell the difference between them because there *was* no difference—not even to Edgar and Allan. One moment one was Edgar, the next he was Allan. Same boy, different identity; same identity, different boy. Their thoughts and actions were not identical but coordinated, like moving parts in a single fine Swiss watch. Each always knew what the other was thinking, feeling, experiencing. Sometimes, they wondered if they were actually one boy with two bodies. Or two boys with one mind.

"*So* sorry to have disturbed your beauty sleep, boys," Mrs. Rosecrans said.

"Oh, that's all right," Edgar said, rubbing his eyes.

"You can just pick up your lecture where you left off and we'll get right back to sleep," Allan added.

The rest of the class laughed.

Mrs. Rosecrans didn't think the matched set of Poes was funny, even if they *were* the most knowledgeable students she'd ever had. "So you two didn't hear a word of what I just said?"

They shook their heads no, in unison.

She waved a note from the main office. "The principal wants to see you both, immediately."

The boys' classmates looked concerned.

But Allan and Edgar just yawned and ruffled their own already unruly heads of hair. "Why?" they asked.

"When it comes to you two, I can't even begin to guess," she answered.

The boys stood and gathered their books.

"Maybe Principal Mann needs our help planning the school's curriculum," Allan said.

"Either that or he wants our help writing his memoirs," Edgar added.

Mrs. Rosecrans pointed to the door.

"Good luck," the boys' classmates whispered.

Edgar and Allan nodded appreciatively, though they didn't think they'd need luck. The principal had always been putty in their hands.

The long hallway that led from Mrs. Rosecrans's classroom to the main office of Edwin "Buzz" Aldrin Middle School was empty aside from a scattering of other students who were excused from class for one reason or another.

"Hey, Edgar and Allan, are you guys going to the principal's office again?" asked perky Sherry George, who was on her knees painting LUNCHTIME PEP RALLY on a ten-foot-long strip of paper.

The boys nodded.

"Does he want to see you about the skeleton?" she continued.

"Could be."

A few days before, the boys had slipped into the

biology lab during lunch period and artfully rearranged all the bones on the human skeleton. The result was a grotesque form that so startled and wrecked poor Mr. Parker's nerves when he returned that he had to postpone that afternoon's exam. The Poes' less academically prepared classmates had been very grateful.

Another voice called from across the hallway, "Pssst, guys!"

It was Stevie "The Hulk" Harrison, one of their best friends, perched uncomfortably on a tiny chair outside Ms. Jenkins's ("No talking will be tolerated!") classroom. He motioned them over. "Does the principal want to see you about the rockets?"

The previous Thursday night, Edgar and Allan had stolen onto their rival school's soccer field and dug half a dozen holes. Into these holes, they deposited six small rockets, covering their handiwork with a thin layer of turf. Late in Friday's game, with the score tied 1-1, the six rockets simultaneously launched, ripping into the sky and bursting at their apex into a spectacular shower of red and gold sparks (Aldrin Middle School's colors). Naturally, everyone gazed skyward—or almost everyone. When the wide-eyed fans, referees, and players eventually returned their attention to earth, they discovered that Stevie "the Hulk," who'd been in on the plan, had just kicked the ball into the net for his first-ever goal, a game-winner, unopposed.

Who knew the two most valuable players weren't on the field but in the stands, putting away their remote launchers?

The twins continued down the hall to more questions: *Could it be this? Could it be that?*

"Could be," the Poes acknowledged every time.

Edgar and Allan had a lot of school spirit.

Mr. Mann stood beside his cluttered desk, his eyes narrowed to slits, his broad chest puffed out like a rooster. "Close the door behind you and don't give me any of your guff," he snarled.

"'Guff'?" Edgar asked.

"It's what you're both full of," Mr. Mann said.

"That's funny," Allan answered. "Last time we were here you told us we were full of 'baloney.'"

"And before that it was 'beans,'" Edgar added.

"And before *that*," Allan said, "you actually told us we were full of—"

"Stop!" Mr. Mann demanded, pointing to two chairs.

They had often seen his face grow red with anger, but at this moment it was a brighter shade than the boys had ever witnessed—something like the color of a baboon's butt. "Sit down."

Allan and Edgar sat.

"Do you boys know the meaning of the word 'incorrigible'?"

"Of course," Allan said.

"'Incorrigible' means to be incapable of being corrected or reformed," Mr. Mann said, ignoring him.

"Yes, it's Middle English from the late Latin," Edgar said.

"*Incorrigibilis,*" Allan added. "From *corrigere,* meaning 'to correct.'"

The principal's mouth opened slightly. "You know Latin?"

The boys looked at each other. "Sort of."

"But we don't teach Latin here," Mr. Mann said. "Have you studied it at home?"

"I wouldn't say 'studied,'" Allan said.

"More like 'played around with,'" Edgar added.

"Dead languages are one of our hobbies," Allan explained. "You know, ancient Greek and Sanskrit . . ."

Mr. Mann was flabbergasted (as usual). Then he

gathered himself. "Never mind about the languages! Your cleverness has never been in question. You two are descended from one of our country's great literary geniuses, so maybe you've inherited something of his proficiency with words, to say nothing of his—"

"His madness?" The corners of Allan's mouth turned up in a slight grin.

"Now, I didn't say that," Mr. Mann countered.

"But you thought it," Edgar said, with an identical smirk.

Mr. Mann shook his head. "You two may know Latin, but you don't read minds."

"That's true," the boys said. Excluding each other's mind . . .

They stood.

"Well, it's been a very pleasant visit, Mr. Mann," Edgar said. "But we should be getting back to class now."

"Yes, it's important we attend to our studies," Allan continued. "But thanks for inviting us to your office. We always enjoy discussing etymology."

The principal's face reddened from the shade of a baboon's butt to that of French teacher Mme. Guimont's lipstick. He clenched his fists. "Sit down right now and behave!"

They sat.

"You boys are incorrigible," Principal Mann repeated, catching his breath.

"If you actually think we're incorrigible . . ." Edgar started.

"Then why are you bothering to talk to us at all?" Allan concluded.

"Because I'm expelling you," he answered.

"What?" Identical expressions of surprise crossed the boys' faces.

"The decision is final," Mr. Mann continued. "We're making special arrangements. You see, you're being expelled from the entire school district. Effective immediately."

WHAT THE POE TWINS DID NOT KNOW . . .

A NOTE RECEIVED THAT MORNING, NOW
FOLDED AWAY IN PRINCIPAL MANN'S WALLET

Dear Principal Mann,

Now that our organization has provided you with evidence against Edgar and Allan Poe, we are confident that you will act in accordance with our wishes. Believe me, you'll never regret removing these troublemakers from your school district.

Sincerely,

Ian Archer

Ian Archer, P.O.E.S.

P.S. I'm sure I needn't remind you that we have also obtained evidence regarding the money you pocketed from your school's funds. However, as long as you do as we wish, you'll have nothing to worry about.

P.P.S. If you ever mention the existence of our organization to *anyone*, we will deliver to you a fate even worse than prison.

A TREACHEROUS FIX

MR. MANN returned to his chair, settled back, and sighed. "Look, boys, we've given you every last opportunity." He nervously wiped sweat from his brow.

What could a principal have to fear? the boys wondered.

"We tried keeping you together in classes, separating you, punishing you, praising you, even letting you teach the advanced material from time to time," he continued, his voice softening. "I know you two haven't had it easy since your mother and father were . . ." He searched for a delicate phrase.

"Lost in space?" Edgar suggested.

Mr. Mann nodded. "Yes, that was very sad."

It *was* sad. Everyone in America knew the story. Mal and Irma Poe, the boys' parents, had been brilliant and dedicated rocket scientists. But seven years before, while making last-minute adjustments to the Bradbury Telecommunications Satellite in the payload section of an Atlas V rocket, they lost track of the countdown and were accidentally launched into space. Their absence on the ground was not noted by Mission Control until after the satellite was in orbit. NASA apologized, but there was no bringing them back. On some clear nights, their orbiting tomb was a visible pinpoint of light among the background of stars.

Since then, the twins had lived with their aunt Judith and uncle Jack Poe, who were good and loving guardians, even if they were largely oblivious to the unusual workings of their nephews' minds.

"Do you boys want to know why we're expelling you?" Mr. Mann asked.

They were curious—but they didn't expect much in the way of a good explanation.

Mr. Mann stood and cracked his knuckles. "I'm expelling you because you cheated on your academic evaluation tests!"

"Cheated?" the boys asked, incredulous.

"Yes, and your cheating will throw our entire school district's otherwise outstanding test results into a questionable light with the state authorities," Mr. Mann

said. He picked up a stack of papers from his desk, shuffling them mindlessly. "It's unforgivable. And considering your previous disciplinary record, it's the last straw.
You're out for good. Done."

Confused, Allan and Edgar looked at one another.
They didn't cheat, ever. Why would they? They didn't
need to cheat to get good grades.

"We don't know how you did it," Mr. Mann continued, dropping the shuffled papers back on his desk. "We
put you at opposite ends of the school and gave you the
tests at the same time—and you still missed the same
three questions out of a possible six hundred. Do you
have any idea of the odds against this? Millions to one."

"The only explanation is that those questions must
have been inaccurately worded," Allan said.

"Otherwise, we'd have both missed zero," Edgar added.

"I don't want to hear your critique of the test!" Mr.
Mann snapped. "I want to know how you cheated."

Obviously, he didn't understand how things worked
with Allan and Edgar, whose knowledge was always
identical, however far apart they were. Two boys, one
mind—one mind, two boys. But Edgar and Allan thought
it very unlikely that the principal could ever grasp the
matter. So they sat back in their chairs and grinned. If

they were going to be expelled, then they might as well have a little fun.

"We must be diabolical geniuses," they said, "to pull off a maneuver like that."

"Exactly," Mr. Mann said, missing the irony.

The boys raised their dark eyebrows. What was to be done about someone this dense?

"So does being expelled from the district mean we can join the French Foreign Legion?" Allan asked the principal.

"Can we finally run for Congress?" Edgar inquired.

"Can we start working as brain surgeons?"

"Do you boys take nothing seriously?" Mr. Mann snapped.

"We take breakfast seriously," Allan answered with utter sincerity.

"It's the most important meal of the day," Edgar said.

Mr. Mann gave them a hard look.

But beneath their joking, there *was* something the boys took seriously about this—they'd miss being around their friends and classmates (and even a few of their teachers). And the timing couldn't be worse.

Next Monday was Halloween, their favorite holiday. Every year since kindergarten, Edgar and Allan had come to school dressed as one or another of their great-great-great-great granduncle's characters (ax-wielding madmen, ominous ravens, skeletal grim reapers . . .). Now that tradition would be broken. They would have launched an impassioned plea to stay in school if at that moment they had not been distracted by a small, redheaded man who suddenly emerged from a shadowed corner of the office.

Had he been here all along? If so, he must have been standing very still, the boys thought.

He wore a well-tailored suit and a skull-shaped earring, and as he drew near, they realized he was even shorter than they were (and they were somewhat small for their age). When he smiled, his teeth flashed a blinding white.

"My name is Mr. Archer, boys."

"Nice earring," they answered without sarcasm. They liked skulls.

Mr. Archer nodded. "I wore it especially for you two."

The boys glanced over to Mr. Mann, whose eyes had gone shifty.

"Leave us," Mr. Archer instructed the principal. "We require a moment's privacy."

Mr. Mann looked surprised. "You're asking me to vacate my own office?"

"Exactly," Mr. Archer said.

Mr. Mann slunk out of the room without another word, closing the door after him.

The boys turned back to the little man. They couldn't help admiring his style.

"Are you from some kind of reform school?" Allan inquired.

"Egad, 'reform school' is such an outmoded term."

Actually, the boys could think of few things more outmoded than the word "egad," a slangy exclamation introduced to the language more than three hundred years ago.

"My institution is oriented more toward research than education," he continued.

Institution?

"You're not talking about a . . . *mental* institution, are you?" Edgar asked.

Mr. Archer laughed and shook his head no. "We've been observing you boys for a long time," he continued. "And we've concluded that this is the moment to take control."

"Control of what?"

"The two of you."

"Hey, nobody controls us," the boys snapped in unison, wondering if they might have overestimated the skull earring as a sign of the man's good character.

"Boys, boys, boys," Mr. Archer said, holding out his small hands in a reassuring gesture. "What I meant was control of your case."

"We're not a 'case,'" Allan said.

"OK, perhaps that's not exactly the right word either," Mr. Archer admitted, his eyes narrowing.

"Maybe you should go back to school to study vocabulary," Edgar suggested.

Mr. Archer's face froze, like a mask, and he fixed the boys with a glare. How could such a small man suddenly seem so big? "Don't mistake my organization for the PTA, boys," he said with a growl.

Edgar and Allan kept silent.

Then Mr. Archer smiled, suddenly friendly again. "Do you boys like science experiments?"

They looked at each other. "Yes, particularly messy ones," they answered cautiously.

Mr. Archer nodded. "Egad! Indeed, we're very 'messy.'"

He moved quickly toward the boys as if to shake their hands, but instead removed something shiny from his jacket pocket—tweezers! In a flash, he reached up and plucked several hairs from each of their heads.

"Ouch!" they shouted, jumping away.

He slipped each sample into its own small plastic bag and tucked the bags into his jacket.

The boys started toward the little man, their faces set in identical expressions of anger. But before they got close enough to snatch back the bags of hair, the office door burst open.

It was Mr. Mann, followed by their uncle Jack and aunt Judith.

"Mr. and Mrs. Poe have arrived a few minutes early," Mr. Mann announced apologetically as he bustled in.

Mr. Archer turned toward the trio of adults and froze. After a moment, he murmured, "Excuse me," and without another word disappeared out the door.

Gone.

"That was Mr. Archer," the principal said to Uncle Jack and Aunt Judith. "Pay him no mind. He's, um . . . a school custodian."

"*Custodian?*" the twins exclaimed, their scalps still stinging.

Mr. Mann brushed past Edgar and Allan to stand behind his desk. "Mr. Archer's profession is neither here nor there, boys."

"Mr. Mann, we're not here to talk about a custodian,"

Uncle Jack snapped. He cleared his throat and began to roll up his sleeves, something he did whenever he was nervous, angry, or both. "Edgar and Allan may create a stir from time to time," he admitted. "But they never really hurt anybody."

"No?" Mr. Mann replied. "What about the time their computer hacking knocked out the electrical grid for the entire city of Baltimore?"

"That was accidental," the boys answered.

"And since then we've forbidden them to use computers or cell phones," Aunt Judith added.

"This isn't about computers." Mr. Mann said, shaking his head ruefully. "It's about cheating on their standardized test."

A tell-tale vein in Uncle Jack's forehead began to pulse. "These boys aren't cheaters!"

Mr. Mann cleared his throat. "Allow me to express my regrets that it's come to this," he said. "Please sit down, Mr. and Mrs. Poe."

Neither Uncle Jack nor Aunt Judith sat. Instead, they took up positions on either side of their nephews.

"As a retired schoolteacher, I understand a lot about standardized testing," Aunt Judith said. The boys had always considered her "a good egg" (and not only because of her shape). Usually her eyes were kind and her voice soft. But now her eyes had narrowed, and her voice had an edge. "As my husband said, these boys do *not* cheat."

"Well, their answer sheets indicate otherwise," Mr. Mann said.

"That's because we're *identical*!" the boys said in unison.

Mr. Mann shook his head. "This has nothing to do with your appearance," he said.

He just didn't get it.

"So what are you proposing, Mr. Mann?" Uncle Jack asked, his patience clearly strained.

"They're kicking us out of the whole school district," the boys answered.

Uncle Jack stared at the principal. *"The whole school district?"*

Sheepishly, Mr. Mann nodded. "Until we can make other arrangements."

"Other arrangements? It sounds like you want to send our nephews, the smartest students your district has *ever seen*, to some kind of reform school!"

"We don't like that terminology," Mr. Mann answered.

Uncle Jack glared at Mr. Mann. "We don't like *anything* about it, whatever you want to call it. And you can bet we're going to talk to the superintendent first thing tomorrow morning!"

Aunt Judith put her arms around the boys. "Let's get your things and get out of here," she said.

Edgar and Allan had never been more proud of their aunt and uncle.

Later in the car, the twins leaned over the front seat.

"Trust us, Uncle Jack and Aunt Judith, we're the victims of some kind of treacherous fix," Edgar said.

"Yeah, it has something to do with an 'institution' dedicated to messy science experiments," Allan continued.

"And unauthorized hair removal," Edgar added.

Uncle Jack and Aunt Judith merely shook their heads—over the years, they'd heard too many tall tales from their nephews.

WHAT THE POE TWINS DID NOT KNOW . . .
ENCRYPTED E-MAIL MESSAGE—**TOP SECRET**

From: archer@The-poes.net
Sent: Tues, Oct. 25, 3:18 pm
To: perry@The-poes.net
Subject: CONTACT

Professor,

I made contact with the twins today as planned and obtained hair samples for final DNA analysis. Oh, how useful the brats will be to our revolutionary project!

The school principal followed our instructions to the letter. The boys will soon be ours for the taking. I await further direction.

Your humble servant,
Ian Archer

P.S. The boys' guardians, Jack and Judith Poe, remain unaware of our interest in their nephews and so should prove no problem to us. I recommend against their elimination at this time.

HOME SCHOOL

THE morning after being expelled, Allan and Edgar lingered over the Denver omelets Aunt Judith set out at breakfast.

Afterward, they played with their black cat, Roderick Usher, whom their mom and dad had brought home as a kitten just two weeks before the launching pad accident that claimed their lives. Roderick meant everything to Edgar and Allan. (It didn't hurt that he was probably the smartest cat in the world.) When Roderick retreated for a morning nap, curling into a ball that concealed the furry white figure eight

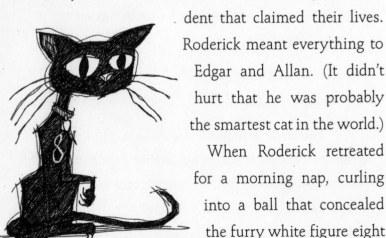

on his chest, the twins turned their attention to a few of the household projects they'd had to put off for the past few weeks.

First they made precise measurements of the shadowy, oddly shaped rooms on the top floor of the large white clapboard house that had been in the Poe family almost back to the days of their famous great-great-great-great granduncle.

They used the measurements to draft a detailed architectural drawing that they hoped would reveal some unaccounted-for space between the rooms, which might indicate a hidden chamber. Who knew what such a chamber might contain?

But no such luck.

Why would anyone build a house like this without a secret

room? they wondered, frustrated by some nineteenth-century architect's lack of imagination.

It was a good thing they had other projects.

Next, they went to the attic, tethering themselves like mountaineers to a crossbeam, and climbed out the small window and onto the steeply angled roof. From here, they enjoyed a good view of the whole neighborhood, though that wasn't the reason they were there. Edgar held a heavy lead ball the size of a baseball. Allan held a lighter lead ball the size of a golfball. The twins had customized each ball with its own built-in stopwatch. Cautiously, they ventured to the edge of the roof and looked straight down into the backyard.

It was a long drop.

In a famous experiment, the sixteenth-century Italian scientist Galileo had dropped cannon balls of different weights from the Leaning Tower of Pisa in order to prove the ancient Greek philosopher Aristotle's theory of motion wrong. Now, Edgar and Allan wondered if they might redeem Aristotle's reputation with new evidence (might some phenomenon of quantum physics have altered the fabric of the universe since Galileo's time?).

"One, two, three," they said in unison, dropping the balls.

After climbing back through the window and un-tethering themselves, they raced downstairs to check the results.

No luck. The speeds proved identical—Galileo re-mained right. The twins had suspected as much, but it would have been nice to make history. Poor Aristotle.

Still, they didn't lose heart.

Instead, they went into the garden to pick asters.

Returning to their uncle Jack's study, they placed the flowers between the pages of two old leather-bound books, flattening the petals. The twins' hypothesis was that a flower pressed in a book of Shakespearean trage-dies would fade in color more quickly than one pressed in a book of Shakespearean comedies. They knew it was a long shot. And that it would take months or even years to determine. But they believed in the scientific method.

"Lunchtime!" their aunt called.

It had been a busy morning, but by the time the twins were seated again at the kitchen table, their thoughts had turned from their experiments to the well-being of their classmates. Who would secretly reprogram the GPS on the school bus next week so that the seventh grade would "accidentally" arrive at a miniature golf course rather than at the sewage plant for their planned (boring) field trip? *If not us, then who?* the boys wondered.

"What's wrong?" Aunt Judith asked.

"Now that we're gone, there's nobody looking out for the kids at school," said Allan.

"Oh, your friends will survive," Aunt Judith assured them as she set out their lunch of peanut butter and jelly sandwiches, apple slices, and snickerdoodles. "The real problem is what we're going to do to educate you two."

"Maybe it's time we went to Harvard," Edgar suggested.

"I don't think being expelled is the sort of recommendation that Harvard's looking for," she answered.

"Then how about if you teach us, Aunt Judith?" Allan asked. "Here at home."

She stopped chewing, letting the words sink in. "What a lovely thought. You know . . . yes, that could work."

"Or we could go to Yale," Allan added.

Aunt Judith laughed and shook her head. "Why don't you boys go outside and spend some time with your friends?"

"It's lunchtime. Our friends are all in school."

"Doesn't the high school get out early today?"

"Well, yes, but . . ."

There were some things Allan and Edgar didn't talk about with their aunt and uncle. They avoided topics that were too brainy—for example, dead languages or advanced mathematics or the microbiology of humming-birds. Nobody could keep up with the twins when it came to such things. And, more important, they avoided any personal topics that might make their guardians feel helpless or sad, keeping quiet about situations they determined were best taken care of by themselves. Things like this:

Many of the older kids were *very* unkind to the Poe twins.

It had been going on for years. Every time the bullies in the neighborhood saw Allan and Edgar, they sang out, "Gruesome twosome, gruesome twosome," pointing and making faces. At first, the boys didn't mind too much. After all, they *were* a twosome, and (as far as they were concerned) there were worse things to be than gruesome. But the lack of originality in the rhyme—"gruesome/twosome"—eventually grated on their literary sensibilities. As poetry, it left a lot to be desired. A first-grader could have done better. And there were even less imaginative names:

> The Twisted Twins
> The Weird Brothers
> The Creepy Couple

The twins knew they were unusual. But what else would they want to be—usual?

Still, it was aggravating.

More recently, "anonymous" kids who left size 11 and 12 footprints in the flower beds had begun to ring the Poes' doorbell every night at the stroke of midnight (neither their aunt nor uncle heard it, because they both wore earplugs to bed). Only after Edgar and Allan wired the ringer to shock anyone who pressed it after 11 p.m. did the prank fall out of fashion.

Next, kids in the same size 11 and 12 shoes toilet-papered the elm tree in the front yard of the Poe house. Not once or twice, but three times. And they'd have continued if Edgar and Allan hadn't connected the sprinkler system to a motion detector they switched on every night before bed.

"On second thought, maybe you ought to stay away from those older boys," Aunt Judith said.

Had she heard some neighborhood talk about the bullies?

She lowered her voice, as if sharing a secret. "Mrs. Ward told me she thinks they're planning to cause even more trouble this Halloween than they did last year."

Worse than last year?

The boys put down their peanut butter and jelly sandwiches.

Last Halloween, the gang had not only egged ten parked cars and stomped to pieces countless carefully carved jack-o'-lanterns but they had also terrorized dozens of little kids who were trick-or-treating, knocking them down and stealing their bags of candy.

This had to be stopped.

Edgar and Allan determined then and there to head off the bullying by exposing these thugs for what they truly were—cowards. To shame them into submission. And now that the twins were temporarily out of school, they had time enough to pull it off. But how? They considered, two minds acting as one.

The bullies needed to be taught a lesson . . .

Halloween was this Monday . . .

The Poe family's old house might be made very spooky indeed . . .

In past years, Allan and Edgar had decorated the front porch for Halloween. This year, they had something more ambitious in mind. They assured Uncle Jack and Aunt Judith that it would all be good fun and that they'd take care of everything themselves—and clean up afterward.

The next afternoon, Edgar and Allan distributed to the smirking clan a hand-lettered, blood-red invitation that read:

SPECIAL HALLOWEEN CELEBRATION
Poe House
The first hour of darkness.
No cowards allowed.

ARE YOU BRAVE ENOUGH?
Probably not . . .

Then they set to work.

Monday night, when the battalion of bullies arrived, Edgar and Allan met them on the porch costumed in funereal shrouds and disguised by corpselike masks daubed with what appeared to be blood—twin versions of the frightening medieval harbinger of doom in their great-great-great-great granduncle's story "The Masque of the Red Death." The two phantoms silently beckoned with rotting fingers toward the front door, allowing their "guests" to enter the house only one at a time.

That's when the fun began.

In the entryway, each bully immediately had to drop to his hands and knees to avoid a huge, swinging scythe that *looked* as if it could take a boy's head clean off.

And it only got worse from there.

Next, each had to crawl through a dark, narrow passage that Edgar and Allan had constructed from fitted rubber sewer pipe. The slimy creatures that felt like worms actually *were* worms, bought at a local bait shop. In the dark, the writhing worms felt extra squishy. Mixed among the worms were long, tangled strands of intestines, mushy lungs and livers, stomach linings, softball-sized hearts, gooey kidneys, and assorted exotic animal glands that the boys had retrieved from refuse bins at a sausage factory near the harbor.

The passage wound through the entryway, across the sitting room, and finally to the basement stairs, which were invisible in the darkness. The unsuspecting older boys tumbled screaming, one by one, into the basement, which Edgar and Allan had turned into a medieval dungeon.

There, recorded bursts of thunder crashed in sync with lightning flashes, while bloodcurdling shrieks filled the air. Authentic-looking ghostly apparitions appeared, some headless and bloody. And scariest of all, there was no visible exit. The boys' guests could do nothing but scramble around like bugs in a jar. Meanwhile, the younger neighborhood kids, some of the boys' classmates, and their friend Stevie "The Hulk" Harrison gathered upstairs, gleefully watching it all on a closed-circuit TV.

Happy Halloween.

Ordinarily, Uncle Jack and Aunt Judith would never have allowed such mayhem, but with all of the recorded sound effects echoing around the neighborhood, they never imagined that the screaming in their basement was real. Besides, the boys eventually released their captives, none of whom had actually been hurt.

Sure, all of them had wet their pants. But what was Halloween for if not to scare the pee out of a few bullies?

Especially if it embarrassed them enough that they didn't show their faces on the street for the rest of the night.

None of the neighborhood's trick-or-treaters was robbed of candy, all the jack-o'-lanterns made it through the night, and nobody had to scrub streaks of egg off their windows or cars.

Best of all, the bullies learned an important lesson about themselves . . . and Edgar and Allan.

"There'll be no more dungeons for you two!" Uncle Jack said when he learned how far they had gone to terrify.

The twins didn't bother to explain all the reasons why they'd done it. Adults almost never approved of such methods, no matter how good the cause. So as the lecture had continued, they simply hung their heads (knowing their uncle needed to think his occasional tirades actually frightened them). And after cleaning it all up, Edgar and Allan hid the painted panels and other horrific props in the rafters of the attic, because they suspected a time might come when reconstructing the dungeon would serve their purposes.

In this, they were not wrong.

ఆ‍♦‍ఌ

Later that week, Aunt Judith announced that she had hired workmen to set up a home school in the basement, the earlier setting of the Halloween horrors.

The result was three days of hammering, sawing, and drilling that Edgar and Allan thought could have been reduced to a more efficient two days' labor (saving their aunt and uncle a few bucks), if only the sweating workmen had been willing to take a little of the twins' advice.

But the carpet layers didn't want to hear about the chemistry of adhesives, the carpenter didn't have the slightest interest in the optimal angle, geometrically speaking, for a miter saw, and the electrician didn't seem to care in the least about the activity of the subatomic particles in the wiring he installed.

Instead, the workmen banned Allan and Edgar from the site (even their friend Stevie Harrison, who came over one afternoon to help build an astrolabe out of old compact discs, was denied access to the basement).

It was a frustrating three days.

But the boys needn't have worried.

At 8:30 a.m. on the second Tuesday of November, Edgar, Allan, and Roderick were allowed to go downstairs. The workmen were gone. In their place waited Aunt Judith, no longer in her morning velour sweatsuit but dressed like a real teacher. One would never guess it was the same person.

Or the same room! Cheerfully lit, the basement had a new carpet, two student-sized desks, one teacher's desk, whiteboards, maps, built-in bookshelves, and an overhead projector—but no computers, because the boys' hacking skills were not to be trifled with.

"Like it, boys?" Aunt Judith asked proudly.

"Well, it's not exactly a lecture hall at Oxford, but it's not bad," Allan said.

As a final brightening touch, Aunt Judith had purchased a set of six posters that featured cuddly animals and cheery sayings. She motioned for the boys to take their seats, and then used a letter opener to slit open the package of posters. Then she took one out, unfolded it, and displayed it.

"Well, what else *could* it be but the first day of the rest of your life?" Edgar asked from a cross-legged position atop his desk.

"It's meant to be encouraging," she answered as she smoothed out the poster.

"What if your life is one of misery?" Allan inquired, identically cross-legged atop *his* desk. "Isn't the first day of yet more misery actually quite depressing?"

"It doesn't work like that," Aunt Judith said in her teacher tone of voice. "The poster refers to each day being a fresh start."

"OK," Edgar said, happy to put off any actual schoolwork. "What if your life has been good up to now and this *new* day is the start of your decline into misery and madness?"

"The poster says nothing about misery or madness!"

"But it doesn't say anything about happiness, either," Allan responded.

"Actually, it doesn't say anything at all," Edgar concluded, standing and taking the poster from his aunt. Carefully, he refolded it into a square no larger than a notebook page. "You should try to get your money back for this one."

Reluctantly, Aunt Judith took the next poster from the package.

"Let's have a look," Allan said.

Edgar nodded. "They're probably all just as bad."

Soon all but the last poster had been opened and then refolded, rejected. Pictures of panda bears, adorable raccoons, and fuzzy puppies spouting sweet, optimistic sayings were all stacked beside the teacher's-edition textbooks on Aunt Judith's desk. However, the final poster in the package was another matter.

"What's this?" she asked, baffled. "They must have made a mistake at the factory."

Like the others, the poster had a picture of a cuddly

animal—this time, a sleeping, fluffy white kitten. Nothing unusual about that. But the words underneath the picture, written in stark, gothic script, suggested neither folksy wisdom nor heartfelt encouragement. In fact, they made no sense at all:

Even Roderick Usher, sitting regally atop a bookshelf beside a paperweight shaped like a raven, looked inquiringly across the room at the nonsensical poster.

"Why would someone beware a cute little cat napping?" Aunt Judith asked. "Sleeping kittens are precious. And they nap all the time." She looked over at the bookshelf. "Right, Roderick?"

Roderick stood and stretched, his expression noncommittal.

After a moment, she shrugged and refolded the poster. "Oh well, it must just be a mistake."

But the boys didn't dismiss it so quickly.

They took a particular (some might say "peculiar") interest in things that others disregarded as mere mistakes, because they believed that oddities and seeming coincidences were actually the world's way of communicating secret messages.

Sometimes these messages were simple to decode. Once, in downtown Baltimore, the boys had noticed a theater marquee on which two of the electrified characters had burned out. A new play about the poet Emily Dickinson, *The Poet's Rule*, was advertised instead on the faulty marquee as:

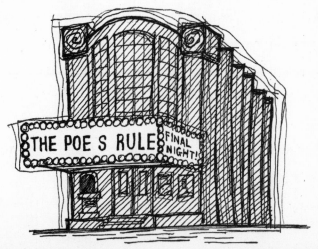

"Darn right we rule," the boys had observed.

Edgar and Allan discovered messages in many places. Broken billboards, half-blown-away skywriting, misprinted lists of ingredients on the backs of cereal boxes. Adults usually categorized such thinking as "overactive imagination." But the boys knew that if you consider everything with an open and inquisitive eye, then at the very least you ensure that the world is never boring.

"OK," Allan mused. "What might this cat poster be trying to say to us?"

"Well, what threat can a sleeping cat pose?" Edgar asked. "Why should one 'beware' it?"

"It's just a misprint, boys," Aunt Judith said.

They weren't so sure.

"Maybe we should ask ourselves to *whom* a sleeping cat might be a threat?" Edgar suggested.

"Of course!" Allan slapped himself in the forehead as if it should have been obvious.

"A sleeping cat is a threat only to a dream mouse," the boys said in unison.

High fives.

"Dream mouse?" Aunt Judith asked, confused. "What's that supposed to mean?"

They shrugged. "Maybe we should ask the rodent

expert," Allan suggested, with a glance at the bookshelf.

"Well, Roderick?" Edgar prodded.

Once again, Roderick Usher was noncommittal.

Aunt Judith clapped her hands in her best teacher style. "All right, enough of this lollygagging." She set the sleeping-kitten poster aside and picked up a sheet of paper from her desktop. "This is a letter from the Baltimore School District." She waved it in the air before flattening it on her desk to read. "It says that in seven days a representative will visit us to evaluate our 'educational environment and processes' in order to give final approval for our home school. It's important, boys. So let's get started."

For Aunt Judith's sake, they sighed and took their seats.

Hours later, upstairs in their room, the twins wrote a note to their former classmates:

The Seventh Grade Class
c/o Stevie Harrison
Edwin "Buzz" Aldrin Middle School
345 Carmello Court
Baltimore, MD 21215

Hi, colleagues,

Since we still aren't allowed to use computers or cell phones (who'd have thought that changing the numbers for every cell phone on the East Coast would be such a big deal?) snail mail will have to suffice. Oh well, it's not as if we have anything very timely to report here at "Aunt Judith Academy." She's doing her best, but it's not exactly Hogwarts.

Anyway, we appreciate the "Save the Poe Twins" petition you all got together, even if Mr. Mann tore it up. Uncle Jack thinks we'll be back in class next school year. That's only ten months away (or seven, if you don't count summer vacation). In the meantime, who's looking out for you guys? And who's keeping things interesting?

If only a little adventure would come knocking on our door. . . . But that only happens in stories, right?

Bye for now,
E and A

WHAT THE POE TWINS DID NOT KNOW . . .

From the Desk of
PROFESSOR S. PANGBORN PERRY, PhD

NOTES FOR EXPERIMENT

a) Recent scientific experiments indicate that a tiny, subatomic particle afloat in space may be paired up with another like particle in such a way that if the two are separated, even by distances as wide as the whole universe, they still remain mysteriously connected. Whatever affects one affects the other, simultaneously. What joins them, even when they're apart? It's a mystery. . . . But it's real. Scientists call it "quantum entanglement." Einstein called it "spooky action at a distance."

b) Now, imagine if the two joined objects were not mere particles but human beings. Two bodies, two locations, but one shared mind. . . . You could send one halfway across the world and the other would still know what his partner was seeing, thinking, doing.

And vice versa. Instantaneous communication . . . Imagine the possibilities for political, scientific, economic, and military power!

THE FOLLOWING IS

THE TRILLION-DOLLAR QUESTION:

What happens if one of the entangled pair of boys is not merely removed from his brother to some distant location on the earth but is killed? Will the remaining boy suddenly know nothing more of his deceased partner? Or, as I believe, will he still be linked to his brother and thereby linked to the mysterious world of the dead, the "afterlife"?

Imagine the power to be gained by controlling the remaining boy and thereby gaining private communication with the next world. The only price for such an endeavor would be the death of one of two boys who are so identical that to kill one would merely be to correct a redundancy. Truly, who needs both Edgar and Allan Poe in our world? Yes, this is the secret purpose of my experiment. To gain control of the two boys, terminate one, communicate with the realm of the dead via the captive brother, and thereby rule both worlds!

At this moment, the plan is proceeding with clockwork precision. . . .

LESSONS IN HORROR

THE boys' homeschooling went well the first week, even if they had to slow down a bit to accommodate their Aunt Judith. Then Roderick Usher went missing.

Edgar and Allan looked everywhere for him, even checking inside the walls to ensure that their poor cat had not somehow been walled up alive, as one of their great-great-great-great granduncle's most famous stories, "The Black Cat," had involved just such a terrifying incident.

But they found nothing.

Allan and Edgar were distraught.

Roderick was special—and not just because he was the last gift their mom and dad ever gave them.

Over the past seven years, Edgar and Allan had taught him many tricks. There was the Stuffed Cat, where he froze on command. (His cue was two lines from one of their great-great-great-great granduncle's poems, "Lo! In yon brilliant window-niche, how statue-like I see thee stand.") Roderick could hold a pose for so long that visitors often mistook him for a work of taxidermy, and their shock when he seemed to come suddenly to life (cued by a finger snap) was very gratifying.

Also, Roderick was born able to imitate the sound of various birds, which proved helpful to his expeditions through the tangled branches of the neighborhood trees. Edgar and Allan added many other sounds to his repertoire, including monkey calls, hissing snakes, crying babies, barking dogs, and whistling teakettles. Who knew when the odd sound effect might come in handy?

But their cat's most useful talent was untying knots with his unusually strong and agile paws. The cue was the twins' whistling "Ring Around the Rosy." The Knot Trick was especially entertaining down at the Baltimore docks, where he was able to fray, unravel, and then unknot even the thickest rope to release moored yachts. The boys loved watching yachtsmen in sport jackets and leather deck shoes toss their cocktails aside and dive into the water to swim after their receding boats.

And Roderick could work wonders with smaller

knots as well, which made him a great help around the house. When Uncle Jack's back was so painful that he couldn't bend over, Roderick untied his sneakers for him. Aunt Judith, a semi-professional knitter, relied on the cat's help whenever a project snarled.

After Roderick disappeared, Allan and Edgar barely slept or ate.

Fortunately, just a few days after the disappearance, Aunt Judith got a phone call with the good news that Roderick had apparently wandered into a delivery truck and survived for days on leftover fast food that the driver had tossed carelessly into the back of the cab.

He was alive and well in Kansas.

What a relief!

Naturally, Aunt Judith offered to pay for Roderick's return via airplane, but the man who had found him refused.

"What's he want, a ransom?" Uncle Jack asked that night at dinner, when he heard the story. "Is he some kind of nut?"

"Not at all," the boys answered. Aunt Judith already had filled them in on the details of her conversation. "He's an animal lover."

"Who is he?" their uncle asked, tucking his napkin into his shirt.

The boys tossed onto the table a brochure that the man had faxed a few hours before. "He's the owner and operator of some kind of *Wizard of Oz*–themed amusement park in Kansas. It's called the Dorothy Gale Farm and OZitorium," said Allan. "It's also his home."

"He goes by the somewhat unoriginal name of Professor Marvel," Edgar added.

"So he *is* a nutcase," Uncle Jack remarked.

"No! He's an animal lover!"

They explained that the professor believed it would be cruel to lock Roderick inside a small cage stowed in the dark belly of an airplane along with luggage and airmail and who-knew-what-else. And the boys agreed. It reminded them of another of their great-great-great-great granduncle's stories, "The Premature Burial," in which a poor soul suffers the horrors of believing he has been buried alive in a coffin. Their cat simply could not undergo such a fearful experience.

"But flying's the best way to travel, boys," Uncle Jack said as he forked a pile of spaghetti onto his plate. "For cats as well as humans."

"Not for *our* cat," Allan answered, stabbing his knife into the rubbery chicken parmesan that sat beside the spaghetti. "Imagine what it would feel like to be locked inside a little box, Uncle Jack. Have you no heart? Imagine being in a coffin, buried under six feet of cold, damp earth."

"Nobody's talking about burying your cat," Uncle Jack replied evenly.

"But putting him in a pet carrier is like walling him into a stone tomb," Edgar said as he picked all the mushrooms out of the sauce on his plate. "Imagine the darkness, the stale air, the frigid chill, the terror."

"So what do you two propose we do?" With a sigh, Uncle Jack put down his fork and picked up the grainy black-and-white fax of the brochure for the Gale Farm and OZitorium. "You want to leave the poor animal with this crazy professor?"

"No," the boys replied. "We want to drive there to pick him up, and then we'll drive him home."

"Drive?" Uncle Jack replied, dumbfounded. "That's thirteen hundred miles away!"

"But Uncle Jack, please—"

"Are you two sure this isn't an excuse to visit this weird amusement park?"

Edgar snatched up the fax and read aloud. "'Visitors will discover on our grounds the actual home of Dorothy Gale, famous heroine of the beloved Oz story.'"

Aunt Judith narrowed her eyes. "How can it be the 'actual' home of Dorothy Gale when she was a fictional character?"

Edgar continued, "'In addition, we offer a live musical production of *The Wizard of Oz*, performed daily.'" He tossed the brochure back onto the table. "Does that sound like someplace my brother and I would *ever* want to visit, Uncle Jack?"

"Actually, yes—it's just the sort of place you two would find funny."

"Just the sort of place where you could wreak havoc," Aunt Judith added knowingly.

"Driving twenty-five hundred miles round trip is out of the question," Uncle Jack declared. "And that's final."

"But Uncle Jack—"

Aunt Judith didn't let them finish. "Can't this discussion wait until tomorrow?" Her voice was uncharacteristically edgy.

"But Roderick—"

"The darned cat'll keep!" Aunt Judith snapped.

Everyone turned toward her, surprised.

She slapped her palms on the table, making the dishes and water glasses jump. "Have you boys forgotten that the representative from the Baltimore School District is coming tomorrow morning to evaluate our home school? To evaluate *everything*?"

Actually, Allan and Edgar *had* forgotten it.

She collected herself. "Tomorrow's too important for us to wear ourselves out arguing about Roderick."

The twins settled back in their seats, their minds working fast:

A representative from the school district . . .

Evaluation . . .

Roderick Usher fifteen hundred miles away . . .

After a moment, identical grins spread across their faces. Suddenly, they weren't worried about any of it— they had a plan.

At breakfast the next morning, the boys assured their nervous aunt that they would be models of good behavior for the school district representative.

It was no lie.

What they did *not* tell her was that in the wee hours

of the night they had snuck out of bed and into the attic. There, by flashlight, they had removed the painted flats and props from their Halloween dungeon, carried them down into the basement, and silently transformed Aunt Judith's spic-and-span "classroom" into something else entirely.

"More pancakes?" Aunt Judith asked the boys, unaware of their handiwork.

Uncle Jack had already left for his morning walk.

"No thanks," Edgar answered, taking a sip of his morning Darjeeling tea.

"You needn't worry about us, Aunt Judith," Allan added, pouring himself a glass of prune juice.

The boys took no pleasure in what they were about to do to her, but what choice did they have?

Roderick Usher needed them.

Aunt Judith looked at her watch. "It's five minutes to eight." She wrung her hands nervously. "The district representative will be here any minute."

The boys dutifully put their dishes in the kitchen sink and told their aunt they would be seated at their desks and hard at work when she and the representative made their way downstairs to the classroom.

The doorbell rang.

"Get downstairs, now," Aunt Judith instructed. "We don't want it to look like we've been waiting. She needs to believe this is a day just like any other."

The boys grinned. "Yes, just like any other."

What the Baltimore School District's Mrs. Antonia Shepard saw when she entered the basement, a steaming mug of tea in her hands, was like nothing she had ever seen or even imagined in her forty-seven years of work. She nearly dropped her tea. "My word, what kind of classroom is *this*?" she exclaimed.

Allan and Edgar sat dutifully at their two desks, just as they had promised their aunt. However, the desks were now at the center of a gruesome, torch-lit medieval dungeon that would have terrified Lucifer himself, to say nothing of a blue-haired school-district employee. To make their conditions appear even more distressing, the boys had smeared Vaseline on their faces, which, in the flickering light, looked like sweat. They panted with exhaustion over piles of printed assignments as thick as phone books, the stubs of pencils clutched in their pale hands.

"What *is* all this?" Aunt Judith's voice was faint with shock.

"We're working as hard and as fast as we can, Aunt Judith," Allan answered, bowing his head again to a page covered with equations.

"We've been at it since sunrise," Edgar said, breathless. "Just like you told us."

"I mean, what's all *this*?" she repeated, gesturing at the classroom turned torture chamber.

"It's academic motivation," Edgar answered.

"'There's nothing like a medieval environment and techniques to inspire a boy,'" Allan said. "Isn't that what you always say, Aunt Judith?"

Mrs. Shepard turned on her angrily. "Don't you think you're working these boys a bit too hard?"

"No, this isn't how it is," their aunt stammered. "You must understand . . ."

The boys muttered something unintelligible, resting their heads on their desks.

Mrs. Shepard went to them. "What is it you're saying, lads?"

"We need a vacation," Edgar whispered, his voice and manner as pathetic as poor Tiny Tim's.

"Indeed you do," Mrs. Shepard answered.

"Maybe a car trip halfway across the country?" Allan proposed, equally pathetic. "Maybe to Kansas?"

"That's a wonderful idea, young man," Mrs. Shepard said. "Fresh air, open spaces." She turned to Aunt Judith, daggers in her eyes.

Aunt Judith nodded slowly, her face pale. "We could do that, I guess."

"You *guess*?" Mrs. Shepard said. "You *must* get these boys out of this . . . this"—she searched for the right word—"this *dungeon* and out into the open!"

"To Kansas?" the boys pressed.

Mrs. Shepard's gaze remained severe.

Aunt Judith sighed, defeated. "It's quite far, but I suppose we can make educational stops along the way. . . ."

Mrs. Shepard nodded.

The boys struggled to keep from smiling

"I'll show Mrs. Shepard out now, boys," Aunt Judith said. "Then I'll be back and we'll *talk*."

The plan had worked perfectly.

Roderick Usher, here we come.

However, their celebration was cut short when they climbed to the basement window to watch Mrs. Shepard leave.

A car awaited her at the curb. After she got in and said a few words to the driver, the car pulled away and the boys caught sight of who was behind the wheel—

the small, redheaded man from the principal's office, Mr. Archer! The hair plucker.

"Hey, what's he got to do with this?" Allan exclaimed.

"Egad," Edgar muttered.

"Some kind of treacherous fix?" But they had no further time to consider the mystery.

"Boys?"

They turned.

Aunt Judith stood at the head of the basement stairs. The boys expected to find an aggravated expression on her face. But that was not what they saw.

Instead, Aunt Judith's eyes were swollen with tears.

The boys' hearts sank. They hadn't actually meant to hurt her. The truth was, they hadn't given her much thought, being so focused on Roderick. Nonetheless, they'd embarrassed her in front of the school official, and their poor aunt didn't deserve that. The boys searched for clever words to make her feel better, but for once they could think of nothing to say or do. They only hung their identical heads.

"I'm sorry, boys," she said.

She was sorry? They looked up.

She looked away. "I got so carried away with the idea of being back in the classroom, a teacher again after all these years, that I forgot how much your cat means to you. He's your best friend, the last present your parents gave to you. I know why you did what you did. I'm so sorry," she repeated. "Don't worry, I'll talk to your uncle about making things right." She wiped the tears away, smiled, and shook her head reflectively. "A medieval dungeon . . .

Oh, Edgar and Allan, you're a pair of wild cards, that's for sure. Jokers."

The boys shared the same thought: *If we're Jokers, then she is the Queen of Hearts.*

But they didn't say anything.

It was sometimes hard for them to tell their aunt and uncle how much they really liked them.

WHAT THE POE TWINS DID NOT KNOW . . .

Mrs. Natasha Perry
Prisoner #89372
State Prison for Women
Senior Citizen Wing
Ossining, NY 10562

ⱱꞦⱧꞨ ⊡ⱮⱱⱱⱤꞨ◖

≈✦ ⊙✳ ⵠⵍꞦⱧⱱ ⱱⱍⵡⱢⵔꞟⱱ ØꞦⱧⵍ✦Ⲥ ⱞ
◖ⱧØ'ⱱ ⱱꞦⵔⴷ ⵔⱢⱱ ⵍꞦⵡⱧⱬ ⱱⱱꞦ ✦ⱱⱱⵍ✳
ⱱⱱⱧⱱ ⵄⵠⵍ✦ⱱ ⵟØ✦ⱭⱭⵍꞦ✦ ⵔꞦ ✦ⱱ ⵔⱧØ✳
✳ꞦⱧⵍ✦ Ⱨⵠⱶ✕ ꞟꞦ⊙Ꞧⵔⵔⵍⱱ ✦ⱱⱶⵄⵟØⵍ ⵔꞦ
ⵍⱱꞦ ⱱⵟⵕⱧⱍⱬ ⱶⵄ ⵄⵕ ⵛⵝ ⵍꞦ★ ⵝꞦ✦Ⲥ
ꞦⱶꞦⱱ ⱱⱱꞦⵝ ⱞ ⵍꞦⴷⵛⵍⱭⵟⱟꞦ✦ ⱱⱱⱧⱱ ⱱⱱꞦ
ⴷⱱⱧⵍⱧⵄⱱⱱꞦⵍ ⱶⵄ ⵄⱱⵛⵄꞦ✦✦ⵛⵍ ⊡ⱧⵍⵔꞦⱬ
(ⱧⵝⱧ ⱱⱱꞦ ⱱⵟ◖Ⱨⱍⱬ✳) ⵏⵛ✦✦Ꞧ✦✦Ꞧⱬ ⱱⱱꞦ
ⵏⵛⱱⱤⵝⱱ◖Ⱨⱬ ⱱⵛ Ꞧⱱ ⱱⱱꞦ ⵔⵍ✦ⱱ ⵏⵛⵝⱤⵍⵉ
ⵄⱢⱬ ⵔⱧØ ⱟꞦ ⱱⱱꞦ ⵛⵍⱍⱬⵛ✕ ⵠⵍØ✦ⱟ‡Ɽⵍ
ⱱⵍⵛ ⱱꞦ ⵔⱧØⵟⵏⱢⵛⱧⱱꞦ‡ ⵍⱱⱱꞦⵍ✦ ⵔ✳
ⵏⵛⵛⱬⵟØⵍ ✦ⱱⵍⱟØⵍ✦ ꞦⱤⱱⱟØ‡ ⱱⱱꞦ ✦ⴷꞦ-

NOTE: *The text of the preceding letter is written in a replacement code to render the communication gibberish to the prison guards or any other reader except its intended recipient. The decoded translation is as follows:*

Dear Mother,

As my great triumph nears, I can't help but recall the story that first inspired me so many years ago. Remember showing me *The Wizard of Oz* on TV? Yes, even then I recognized that the character of Professor Marvel (aka the Wizard) possessed the potential to be the most powerful man in the world. Consider how he manipulated others by pulling strings behind the scenes. He ruled an entire city and held the whole land in fear and awe of him. However, he lacked killer instinct, and so in the end he merely floated away in a pathetic balloon. (Oh, why didn't he just kill Dorothy and her friends when he had the chance?) Still, he *was* my inspiration and he remains my namesake now that I'm in hiding, but I will not make his mistake. I do *not* lack the killer instinct. You'll soon see. Hope the prison food still agrees with you.

Regards,
Your Son

Mr. Poe in the Great Beyond

The famous author Edgar Allan Poe tied his silk cravat around his neck and glanced into the office restroom mirror. He brushed his fingers through his thinning black hair. He had to admit that he looked pretty good, considering he'd been dead now for more than a century and a half. Maybe even better than he'd looked when he was actually alive, struggling to make a living from his writing.

Here, one didn't have to worry about money. Still, everyone was gainfully employed. One would go crazy with boredom otherwise. Some folks speculated that Heaven was the only place you could actually be idle and remain happy. This wasn't Heaven. It was more of an "in-between" place.

Mr. Poe had no complaints.

He liked his job. Why not? He still got to be a writer. During his lifetime he'd gotten his fill of writing short stories, poems, essays, and book reviews. He didn't miss "high literature." Well, not much. No, his new job, writing the fortunes for fortune cookies, was fine. It taught him how to be concise. And it was important work, especially as Mr. Poe sometimes put a few of those fortunes to special uses, which he kept secret from his ever-prying boss, Mr. Shakespeare, who disapproved of any contact between those here in the afterlife and those still living.

What are rules for if not to be broken?

Besides, how else was Mr. Poe to help his great-great-great-great grandnephews, his namesakes, who scurried about the Earth below making trouble for those who deserved it and making life more interesting for everybody else? Edgar and Allan were not ordinary boys. For reasons that even Mr. Poe did not understand, the boys' thoughts and feelings were tied to each other. But it was not just this unusual characteristic that sustained Mr. Poe's interest. He admired their adventurous spirit, their darkly perverse sense of humor, and their disregard for any rules that were mere foolishness. Ah, what he'd give to be young and brilliant again and living outside the boundaries set by society. What on Earth—or in this in-between place—could be finer?

Yet all was not well for his nephews.

For years, Mr. Poe had observed a murderous, power-mad professor of quantum physics spying on Edgar and Allan. Now the professor was using a false name and plotting to kidnap the boys for some kind of scientific experiment. Though Mr. Poe wasn't clear on the details, he knew he had to bend office rules to help the boys as best he could.

After a last glance in the mirror, Mr. Poe returned to his cubicle, which was always messier than Emily Dickinson's, but never quite as messy as Walt Whitman's. Mr. William Shakespeare stood waiting for him, arms crossed and an angry expression on his pale, oval face.

This behavior did not intimidate Mr. Poe.

With a few lucky breaks when he was alive, Mr. Poe might have been an even greater poet than Shakespeare.

"But soft! what light through yonder window breaks?" he said to Mr. Shakespeare, moving around his desk and taking his seat.

"Enough of your guff, Mr. Poe."

Mr. Poe wondered if it was those starched Elizabethan

collars Mr. Shakespeare insisted on wearing that made him so irritable. No matter. Mr. Poe leaned back in his chair and put his boots up on his desk, lacing his hands behind his head as if he were merely contemplating a summer day. "Guff?" he asked, in the same mocking tone his nephews had used with their principal.

Mr. Shakespeare ignored him. "Poe, I'm missing a book from my personal library. It's a text on quantum entanglement. Marvelous stuff. Indeed, this new science seems to prove once and for all what I proposed more than four hundred years ago—that there are 'more things in heaven and earth... than are dreamt of in your philosophy.'"

Mr. Poe hated it when Mr. Shakespeare quoted himself.

"Let me assure you, losing a book is quite unusual for me," Mr. Shakespeare continued, fiddling with his tight collar. "Why, I haven't misplaced a volume from my personal collection since . . . well, since I 'accidentally' dropped *your* first book of poems into the office furnace here when you were just a beginning scribbler down in Baltimore." He smirked. "Anyway, you wouldn't happen to know what's become of the book, would you?

Not your book of 'poems,' that is. The expert, critical judgment of the flames took care of that. But my missing book on quantum physics?"

Mr. Poe felt his anger rise. " 'Judgment of the flames,' my derriere!" he thought. His first book of poems had been good. And yes, Mr. Poe had borrowed the science text from Mr. Shakespeare's office. At this moment it sat on a shelf not two feet from where Mr. Shakespeare stood. Anyone could see it. (Though in one of Mr. Poe's stories, "The Purloined Letter," his detective solved a case by realizing that sometimes the most effective place to hide something was in plain sight.)

"Perhaps you can consult one of your old plays to locate the missing book," Mr. Poe suggested snidely. "After all, to hear you tell it, your writing contains all the wisdom of the ages."

Mr. Shakespeare laughed. *"Please.* I'd never say such a thing about my own work. It's only countless generations of scholars who heap such praise upon me."

Mr. Poe sighed. He too had plenty of fans among the critics. Perhaps not as many as Mr. Shakespeare, but then Mr. Shakespeare had been in the public eye for well over two centuries longer than Mr. Poe. Still, there was no use arguing with the boss. Mr. Poe pointed to the book.

Mr. Shakespeare nodded and picked it up. "There's something else, Mr. Poe."

There always was.

"Of equal importance to me," Mr. Shakespeare continued, "is learning why *you've* suddenly become fascinated with this new science."

"I'm a man of diverse interests."

"Yes, but isn't it also true that your nephews are at this moment being menaced by a secret organization whose ambitions have something to do with this subject?"

A question to which Mr. Shakespeare already knew the answer. . . .

"If you've been researching this subject with the intention of somehow getting involved in the boys' dilemma," Mr. Shakespeare said, "then I must remind you that it is not our place to interfere in the lives of those below, however dangerous their situations. Understand?"

"I understand that's the policy," Mr. Poe said.

"And do you plan to abide by it?"

Mr. Poe glanced at his pocket watch. "Ah, I see it's time for my coffee break, Mr. Shakespeare." He swept his boots from his desk and stood. "If you'll excuse me, please."

"You've only been at your desk three minutes, Mr. Poe."

"Is that all? Funny, it seems as if I've been sitting here listening to you for hours and hours."

"Mr. Poe, your attitude is not likely to get you promoted upstairs anytime soon."

Mr. Poe shrugged.

"And there's yet another thing," Mr. Shakespeare said.

"Isn't there always?"

Mr. Shakespeare continued. "Mr. Picasso in the art department just told me that you were recently seen hanging about his poster room. He further explained that a poster with a picture of a sleeping kitten was released with an unapproved, altered message, and that this poster just happened to make its way into the home of your nephews."

"Well, isn't that a coincidence?" Mr. Poe observed, folding his arms across his chest.

Mr. Shakespeare stamped his foot. "You imbecile! Didn't you know that unauthorized transmissions from our world to the world of the living often become garbled? Typographical errors? Lines cut short, words printed backward, or whole passages upside down?"

Mr. Poe shrugged. "Nothing's perfect."

"Imperfection is precisely why we prohibit communiqués."

"I'll keep that in mind in the future, boss."

Mr. Shakespeare shook his head. "Exactly what message do you think you sent down to your nephews on that poster?"

There was no use lying, Mr. Poe figured. "Beware the catnapping."

" 'Catnapping' as one word?"

"Of course," Mr. Poe said. "That terrible professor was plotting to steal their cat. They needed to be warned."

Mr. Shakespeare put his hand to his forehead. "The message went through with an extra space. Instead of 'catnapping,' it read 'cat napping,' Mr. Poe. Two words. You managed only to warn your nephews to beware sleeping cats!"

Mr. Poe's face paled at the news.

ON THE ROAD WITH THE POES

THE Poe family's car trip to Kansas proceeded for hundreds of miles with little to report besides occasional stops for gasoline and a few nights spent in roadside motels. The hours passed easily for Edgar and Allan, who sat in the backseat of the family's Volvo wagon reading their favorite series, True Stories of Horror. Each boy absorbed not only the content of the book in his own hands, but also whatever his brother was reading. As their two sets of eyes scanned two sets of pages, their shared minds were flooded with twice the ideas and images—a fantastic combination of ax-wielding lunatics, vengeful ghosts, mad scientists, mythical monsters, and evil spirits.

But just west of St. Louis, a problem arose.

Edgar and Allan were coming to the last few pages of their last two books.

"Over there!" Allan called, unbuckling his seat belt and tapping frantically on Uncle Jack's shoulder.

In the distance, the boys had spied a shopping center. They saw the signs for a giant electronics store, a giant sporting-goods store, a giant toy store, and, most important, a giant bookstore with escalators, a DVD section, a café, and many books, including the entire sixty-two-volume True Stories of Horror series—or so they hoped.

"Pull over, Uncle Jack. We need more books," Allan said.

Uncle Jack's eyes remained focused on the road ahead. "Why don't you two just trade books with each other?"

The boys rolled their eyes.

"Actually, I could use a bathroom break, Jack," Aunt Judith said.

Uncle Jack nodded and got off at the next exit. "Fifteen minutes," he said as he parked.

Once inside the bookstore, Aunt Judith bee-lined for the women's restroom, Uncle Jack headed for the magazines, and the boys went to the information desk, where a tall blonde woman (nametag: Jeanine) tapped on a keyboard. When she turned to look at the boys, she took off her jeweled reading glasses, letting them drop and dangle from the equally jeweled chain around her neck.

"Hey, you two are twins," she said.

Allan and Edgar did not dignify the comment with an answer. "Do you have the True Stories of Horror series, specifically numbers twenty-four through—"

"And hey," she continued, "you look just like that famous writer."

This happened from time to time.

"You know the one," she continued, pointing to the poster-sized caricatures of famous writers that hung on the walls of the giant store.

Though the boys were eager to get their hands on the new books, they couldn't pass up an opportunity for a little fun. "William Shakespeare?" Edgar suggested.

"No," she answered.

"Walt Whitman?" Allan inquired.

"Yeah, maybe," she said, turning to the bearded caricature of Whitman on the wall above the literature section. "Wait, no. It's somebody else."

"Emily Dickinson," Allan suggested innocently.

Shakespeare   *Whitman*   *Dickinson*

"No, I'm not kidding, boys. You two look like, hmmm . . ." She turned and scanned the caricatures on the opposite wall. "There he is! Up there. Edgar Allan Poe."

She turned back to the boys. "Wasn't he the horror one?"

Edgar nodded. "'The Pit and the Pendulum.'"

"'The Tell-Tale Heart,'" Allan added.

"'The Premature Burial,'" Edgar continued.

"'The Masque of the Red Death.'"

Jeanine made a face. "Oh, I read those stories in high school. I didn't like them. They were too . . ." She searched for the word.

"Too scary?" Allan suggested.

"No. They were too . . ." At last, she found it: "Unrealistic."

The boys were shocked. *Unrealistic?* Who was this woman to criticize their great-great-great-great granduncle?

"I like stories that are more *real*," she continued. "I mean, all that horror stuff . . . those dark and stormy nights, interrupted only by flashes of lightning and screaming? Come on, that never happens."

The boys' eyes burned into her. "You don't believe in dark and stormy nights, interrupted by flashes of lightning and screaming?"

"Well, *I've* never seen one."

Edgar and Allan looked around the store—neither Uncle Jack nor Aunt Judith was anywhere to be seen. Identically wicked grins spread across their faces

"May I see that computer keyboard?" Edgar asked.

She shook her head. "That's against the rules."

"It's not like we're asking for your password to operate it," Allan said reassuringly.

"We just want to *see* it."

She smirked, turning the keyboard around on the counter. "If you two can guess my password, go for it."

Big mistake.

For Edgar and Allan, passwords existed only to be passed by. They cracked their knuckles, masters of making computers do their bidding. They typed a four-handed series of commands (both tap-tap-tapping at once on the keyboard), which injected into the cyber world their wickedly playful imaginations. Of course, they did so strictly for the sake of their great-great-great-great granduncle's literary reputation.

After a moment: ZAP!

The boys stepped away from the keyboard, their hair standing on end as the massive bookstore suddenly filled with static electricity.

The lights flickered. "Hey, what's happening?" Jeanine asked.

The lights went out, sending the vast building into almost total darkness.

Then there was a flash and a boom, like lightning and thunder—but indoors. Was this a meteorological miracle? No, it was a set of ceiling lights flashing on for a split second with such an intense brightness that the bulbs blew out—boom! Then another set and another, exploding in flashes and bursts.

It wasn't quite lightning and thunder. But it *seemed* like the storm of the century.

The escalators started moving at three times their normal speed, changing directions every ten feet. Ten feet up, ten feet down, ten feet up, ten feet down . . . up, down, up, down, up, down. Those customers who were trapped on the terrifying thrill ride could only hold tight to the handrails, their bloodcurdling shrieks slicing through the darkened store.

Meantime, the espresso machines in the café started steaming crazily, hissing like dragons. Cash-register drawers rattled open and closed and credit-card machines beeped and whined like demons. Screaming voices came from more than just those trapped on the lunatic escalators.

Darkness, lightning, screaming . . .

After sixty seconds, the backup lights came on and everything returned to normal—except, of course, for the customers and employees. Many of them still cowered on the ground between the bookshelves. And no one was more frightened than Jeanine, who'd crumpled behind her information desk.

Sometimes defending great literature required extreme measures.

The twins leaned over the counter.

Jeanine remained crouched on the floor, her hands covering her head.

"What do you think now of the darkness and lightning and screaming in Edgar Allan Poe's stories?" Edgar asked, his static-electrified hair still standing on end.

She looked up and tried to rise, but her legs were shaking too much.

"Do you still think they're 'unrealistic'?" Allan inquired.

Unable to speak, she meekly shook her head no.

The twins went behind the counter and helped her up, placing her shaky hands on the counter so she could balance herself.

"Jeanine, you don't have to look up those books for us," Edgar said.

"Yeah, I wouldn't touch that computer for a few minutes," Allan added as they walked away.

A five-year-old boy carrying a Dr. Seuss book tugged with his free hand on Edgar's arm.

The twins turned to him.

"That was the coolest thing I've ever seen," the kindergartner said, grinning as wide as a jack-o'-lantern.

"Glad you liked it," they answered, patting him on the head.

Moments later, Uncle Jack and Aunt Judith found their nephews in the Horror section.

"Did you two do that?" Uncle Jack demanded, walking up behind them.

"Do what?" the pair asked innocently.

Uncle Jack started rolling up his sleeves and fixed them with his most stern expression (which they rated a mere 3.5 on their 1 to 10 "sternness" scale). "Boys, I wasn't born yesterday," he said. "Don't deny it."

"OK, we don't deny it," Edgar said, looking around the wrecked bookstore.

"But you should be pleased with us, Uncle Jack and Aunt Judith," Allan said. "You're always talking about the value of education. Well, today we taught a bookseller a valuable lesson about literature."

"There'll be no new books for you today," Uncle Jack announced as he steered them out of the store.

"What?" they moaned. (The truth was, while reprogramming the computer, they'd checked the inventory and discovered the store was out of the books they wanted. But they kept this news to themselves.) They looked at each other, their eyes puppylike and sad. "No

True Stories of Horror?" they muttered. "Gee, Uncle Jack. You're so mean."

Uncle Jack stood a little taller and nodded as he held open the door for his wife and nephews. "You got *that* right. Now, how about some lunch?"

"Chinese?" Allan suggested.

"Why not?" Now that Uncle Jack had been "stern" enough, he could afford to be generous.

Chinese was the twins' favorite, not so much for the food but the fortune cookies. Or rather, the fortunes inside the cookies.

The Poe family walked across the parking lot to the Jade Dragon. There, they ordered spicy-hot beef, orange chicken, fried rice, and the Buddhist's Delight vegetable plate. The food proved forgettable. But the identical message each boy discovered in his fortune cookie proved otherwise:

The farm is a brilliant trip.

Of course, that meant the Gale Farm and OZitorium.

Uncle Jack and Aunt Judith received ordinary fortune cookie fortunes: "You will share the gift of friendship" and "Your hard work will be rewarded."

"Did you boys get identical fortunes again?" their uncle inquired, looking over their shoulders.

They nodded. They *always* got identical fortunes. Why wouldn't fortune cookies predict the same future for two boys who were virtually interchangeable?

"Twin messages again for our twin boys," said Aunt Judith. "Isn't it amazing how that always happens? What a coincidence!"

Allan and Edgar didn't believe in coincidence.

Rather, they believed in fortune. Particularly when it was packaged in a cookie. . . .

Most people don't take fortune cookies so seriously. But the boys' fortunes had always been accurate. For example, at age five, they each received a fortune that read:

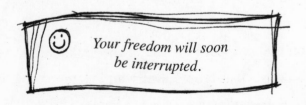

Your freedom will soon be interrupted.

This proved true a few days later, when they found themselves involved in a new enterprise called kindergarten.

At age eight their cookies read:

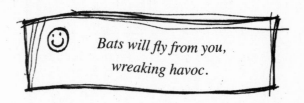

Bats will fly from you, wreaking havoc.

And within a week, both boys were banned from Little League for their inability to hold on to their baseball bats when they were up at home plate. Oh, how the spectators in the stands dodged for cover.

At age ten they read:

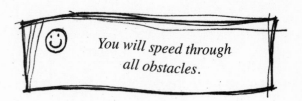

You will speed through all obstacles.

And two days later when the boys "borrowed" Uncle Jack's car for an experiment, they discovered that pressing on the gas pedal instead of the brake indeed renders obstacles such as fences, walls, and plate-glass windows passable. Yes, they sped right through.

And there were many other instances.

Now this: *The farm is a brilliant trip. . . .*

The boys had thought they were just retrieving their cat, but perhaps a few pleasant surprises awaited them.

꧁ ☠ ꧂

WHAT THE POE TWINS DID NOT KNOW . . .

FROM A LETTER WRITTEN NINE YEARS
EARLIER BY THE BOYS' MOTHER, IRMA POE,
TO HER SISTER-IN-LAW, JUDITH

. . . the twins remain the great joy of our lives, even if neither Mal nor I truly understand what makes them tick. Doctors agree they're quite unusual. It's not just that they're such accomplished talkers—lots of three-year-olds talk a blue streak. And it's not just that they're reading every grown-up book they can get their little hands on. What's unusual is that they both <u>write</u> in complete sentences. At three years old! Recently, they've begun experimenting with various poetic forms, like the sonnet. Where does that come from? And stranger yet is that even Mal and I still can't tell them apart. It's not for lack of attention. Believe me, we love our boys. But they confound us. That's why we've agreed to let a specialist at the university observe them. His name is Professor Perry and he's taken an interest. We don't see any downside to his involvement, do you?

Love to you both from
Irma **and Mal**

TALES OF MYSTERY AND IMAGINATION

A bell chimed in the front office of the Wagon Wheel Motel as the road-weary Poe family entered. It had been eight hours since their lunch at the Chinese restaurant and three hours since dinner at a greasy spoon this side of the Kansas border. Now they were only a hundred and ten miles from the Gale Farm and OZitorium. But Edgar and Allan didn't press to go any farther—the hour was late and Uncle Jack was bleary-eyed despite all the coffee he'd been drinking to stay awake.

Roderick would be OK with the professor for one more night.

The motel office was packed tight: a wall of brochures for local tourist attractions, a spinning rack of postcards, two armchairs arranged around an end table with a coffee maker, porcelain coffee mugs, and a pink box of doughnuts (left over from that morning's free continental breakfast). More surprising was a handwritten sign at the tall front desk. It read:

The night clerk, a sleepy man in his early twenties with bad teeth and a ponytail, emerged from the back room carrying a book of Sudoku puzzles. "Can I help you?"

"Hey, we're Poes," Uncle Jack said, pointing to the sign. "Does that mean we get a discount?"

"Twenty percent," the night clerk said, setting the book on the counter.

"How thoughtful," Aunt Judith remarked. "But why for Poes?"

Uncle Jack didn't wait for the answer. "Doesn't matter why," he said, reaching for his wallet. "A discount's a discount. Right? It's a great deal. We'll take it."

"How'd you know we were coming?" Allan asked the clerk.

"Oh, our discount is always available. We value education."

"What does education have to do with it?" the boys asked.

The man looked at them. "You two are good students, right?"

"Depends on what you mean by 'good,'" Allan answered.

"We know plenty of things," Edgar added. "More than our teachers, generally."

The clerk turned to Uncle Jack. "You'll have to show documentation to prove you're a POE."

"No problem." He displayed his driver's license.

"Your *name's* Poe?"

"Sure is."

The man laughed. "I hate to disappoint you, but the discount isn't for people *named* Poe. It's for members of the organization Parents of Exemplary Students. Get it? P-O-E-S. So unless you've got a copy of their current report cards, along with two letters of recommendation from teachers, I'm afraid I can't give you the discount."

Jack balked. "What?"

"But they *are* exemplary students," Aunt Judith said.

"That's true," Allan added, "if by 'exemplary' you not only mean smart but also 'expelled.'"

The night clerk shook his head, a smile still playing on his face.

"Fine, then we'll take our business elsewhere," Uncle Jack snapped, glancing around the cramped office. "This place isn't exactly the Ritz."

The man shrugged. "There's not another motel open for sixty miles."

Aunt Judith tapped her index finger on the counter. "I think this POES organization is a bad idea. My goodness, parents of exemplary students already get many advantages. What about having an organization for parents of *ordinary* students?"

"We tried that," the night clerk said, fighting off a yawn. "We called it Parents of Ordinary Students. But nobody wanted to join, even for the discount."

"Why not?"

"Who wants to be in an organization called the POOS?"

Uncle Jack didn't want to hear any more. "Enough. We'll take two adjoining rooms."

Allan and Edgar turned away and walked over to

the postcard rack. They started to spin it, attempting to identify the greatest possible velocity at which centrifugal force would not send the cards flying off into every corner of the office. Faster, faster, faster . . .

"Wait a minute, your names wouldn't happen to be Edgar and Allan, would they?" the night clerk called out.

The boys stopped spinning the rack (though the rack continued spinning for some time without them) and returned to the front desk. They peered over the top. "Yes, we're Edgar and Allan."

"How did you know their names?" Aunt Judith asked.

"Somebody found a book this morning on the table here next to the doughnuts," he answered. He disappeared under the front desk. The Poes could hear him rummaging around. "I could swear those were the authors." More rustling among junk. "Let's see, it's got to be around here somewhere. Ah! Here it is." He stood up and showed them the book.

"Oh, this explains it," Uncle Jack said. He read the title aloud. "*Tales of Mystery and Imagination* by Edgar Allan Poe. This book's written by Edgar Allan Poe, the famous author. Not Edgar *and* Allan Poe."

The clerk narrowed his eyes. "But look what it says inside."

Uncle Jack opened the book.

Edgar *and* Allan Poe? Uncle Jack and Aunt Judith looked at each other.

"Oh, that's just a misprint," Uncle Jack said.

"A typo," Aunt Judith added. "A coincidence."

But the boys didn't believe in coincidence.

Edgar took the book.

"We'd like to keep it," Allan said.

"Haven't you two already read that?" Aunt Judith asked.

Naturally they had. And while some of the words their great-great-great-great granduncle used were old-fashioned, the stories were grievous, shuddersome, and horrific—in other words, perfect. The twins thought "The Black Cat" had the ideal plot, "The Masque of the Red Death" was outstandingly spooky, "The Pit and the Pendulum" utterly frightening, "The Cask of Amontillado" . . . well, Edgar and Allan thought that every story in the book was the best of one thing or another.

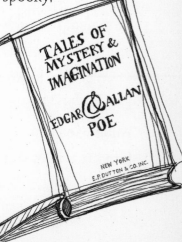

"We'd like to read it again," they said.

But there was more to it than that.

Fifteen minutes later, Edgar and Allan sat cross-legged in their motel room on one of the two beds. The other bed was already a shambles, its covers and blankets tossed and scattered and the mattress crushed in the middle as a result of the boys using it like a trampoline, testing the elasticity of the memory foam and the torque of the box springs. The ceiling above the bed had been cracked by Edgar's head—no damage done, as Edgar's head was quite hard.

Now the boys held the book between them. It was heavy in their hands.

"This clearly contains a special message for us," Allan said.

"Yes, but if you consider all the writing in it, there are thousands of messages," Edgar observed.

"So how do we figure it out?"

Whoever had left it behind had used a tourist brochure, like those in the motel office, as a bookmark. The volume opened to a story called "The Purloined Letter." It began with a short quote in Latin:

Nil sapientiae odiosius acumine nimio.

Of course they knew the translation: "Nothing is more hateful to wisdom than excessive cleverness."

They looked at each other.

"That can't have anything to do with us," Allan said.

Edgar agreed. "We're clever, but not *excessively* clever."

"Actually, we're just clever enough."

They kept reading.

"The Purloined Letter" was one of their great-great-great-great granduncle's most famous stories. In it, a detective is challenged to locate a valuable stolen letter that has been hidden in a particular room. Experts have already searched the room, tearing it apart but finding nothing. The detective immediately realizes that the letter must be hidden in plain sight. And he is right—there it is, in a rack full of visiting cards below the mantelpiece, not hidden at all. Simple! And yet only a genius would think to look in the open for a "hidden" object.

Just as only a genius would look in the open for a "hidden" message.

The twins looked around the room for whatever wasn't hidden.

The problem was that *everything* they saw wasn't hidden.

"It's not so easy when you don't know what you're looking for," Edgar said to his brother.

Nil sapientiae odiosius acumine nimio, they thought.

"Yes, maybe we *are* being 'too clever,'" Allan said.

"OK, so what's the most obvious thing in this room that the message of 'The Purloined Letter' is pointing us to?" Edgar asked.

They looked again at the open book.

Why had it opened to that particular story?

The bookmark!

Might the tourist brochure be more than just a bookmark? Might it be the actual object they were supposed to notice? Might it be the "purloined letter," the message? They set the book down and picked up the brochure:

THE AUTHENTIC
DOROTHY GALE FARM & OZITORIUM

Coincidence? No way.

The boys recalled the grainy, black-and-white fax from Professor Marvel that their aunt Judith now had in her purse. This glossy, full-color brochure had a different headline: THIS YEAR CELEBRATING THE CENTENNIAL OF L. FRANK BAUM'S CLASSIC, *THE WONDERFUL WIZARD OF OZ*! Edgar and Allan knew the vital facts about most major American books, so they knew in a flash that this brochure dated back twelve years.

Edgar read aloud: "'Visitors will discover on our grounds no mere reproduction of the home of Dorothy Gale, famous heroine of the beloved Oz books, but the *actual* house that Dorothy inhabited . . .'"

Same baloney as the fax.

"Wait, look there," Allan said. He pointed to one of the photographs, which had been taken at the entrance to the OZitorium, a small, ordinary-looking theater. It showed a smiling group of tourists—among them, a young man and woman each holding an identical infant. The couple bore more than a mere resemblance to Mal and Irma Poe.

"Is it them?" Edgar asked.

"It looks like them."

stay for a day!

"Then that would make the babies in the photo—"

"Us!"

For a moment, the boys were silent.

"Gee, Mom and Dad sure look happy here," Edgar said quietly.

"Too bad we can't remember being with them that day," Allan said in a small voice.

"Yeah."

Edgar looked at Allan.

Allan looked at Edgar.

Each had one small tear in the corner of his right eye.

After a heartbeat or two, the boys wiped them away.

"Look what it says underneath the picture," Allan remarked.

"Cool," they said.

Later that night, they took from the desk drawer in their room a complimentary Wagon Wheel Motel postcard (photographed decades before, when cars had tailfins and chrome bumpers) and wrote to their friends:

To all,

So far, life on the road is pretty interesting. And every mile brings us closer to our cat, Roderick, who was accidentally transported to Kansas. Along the way, we've decoded a few signs from the Universe . . . you all know how that works, right? Well, maybe not, but trust us—all signs are good.

Most sincerely,
E and A

P.S. Before we left Baltimore we heard from Stevie "The Hulk" Harrison that Mr. Parker can't put the skeleton back together! Maybe now he won't grade quizzes quite so heartlessly.

The Seventh Grade
Aldrin Middle School
345 Carmello Court
Baltimore, MD 21215

WHAT THE POE TWINS DID NOT KNOW . . .

LETTER SENT SEVEN YEARS EARLIER FROM THE
BOYS' FATHER TO PROFESSOR S. PANGBORN PERRY

MAL POE

Space & Aeronautical Design Specialist

Dear Professor Perry,

My wife and I have followed your recent criminal trial and we are glad to know you have been found not guilty. Nonetheless, what a terrible shock it must be for you to learn that it was your own mother who strangled your landlady. What a sad, sad story. You have our sympathies.

However, in light of your recent dismissal from the university, we must now insist that you stop studying our twin sons. Over the past few years my wife and I have come to doubt your methods, particularly your need for secrecy in all your observations.

Please do not mistake the friendliness of this letter for indecision or weakness on our part. Likewise, be assured that while my wife and I may be somewhat busy next week with the launch of the Bradbury Telecommunications Satellite, we will nonetheless set everything aside to ensure our twins' safety. So stay away from them, forever.

Sincerely,

Mal Poe

Mr. Poe in the Great Beyond

Mr. Shakespeare burst into Mr. Poe's cubicle. "A pox on you, Poe!"

Mr. Poe looked up from his desk. "Well, good afternoon to you, too, Mr. Shakespeare."

"I'll have you know that my afternoon has not been 'good' and yours is going to be even worse," Mr. Shakespeare replied.

Mr. Poe put down the pages he'd found that morning in his in-box. They listed the ordinary fortune-cookie fortunes he'd written this past week. Every one had been rejected by Mr. Shakespeare and his editorial committee.

Mr. Poe was not surprised they'd turned down "Your corpse will wither and rot" or "The conqueror worms are hungry for you." He had expected such squeamishness. Nonetheless, he'd been disappointed that they also passed on some of his more optimistic fortunes, such as "Death will come for you soon, cheerfully." What was objectionable about cheerfulness?

He had planned to take the matter up with Mr. Shakespeare. However, judging from his boss's current mood, this seemed like the wrong moment.

"Did you send more communications to your nephews?" Mr. Shakespeare cried.

Mr. Poe shrugged. "'There is nothing either good or bad, but thinking makes it so.'"

Mr. Shakespeare stamped his foot in rage. Nothing got under his skin like having his own quotes used against him. Nonetheless, he pulled himself together. "Exactly what message did you send down?"

There was no use lying. "'The farm is a brilliant trap.'"

"*Trap?*" Mr. Shakespeare put his hand to his forehead. Then he removed from the pocket of his sixteenth-century doublet a copy of the message that had actually gone through.

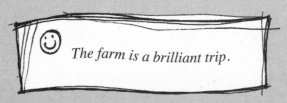

☺ *The farm is a brilliant trip.*

"'Trip' instead of 'trap'?" Mr. Poe muttered, worried.

"A typographical error of just one letter and look what you've got. What you intended as a warning becomes the opposite."

"Oh, no," Mr. Poe whispered, wringing his hands. "One little mistake..." Then he stopped, his expression brightening. "Still, all may not be lost."

"You also did something with a brochure and a book, true?" Mr. Shakespeare accused.

Mr. Poe nodded. "Thankfully, that should straighten everything out."

"*What*, exactly, did you do?"

Mr. Poe was proud of his cleverness. "I slipped an old brochure for the Gale Farm and OZitorium between the pages of my classic story 'The Purloined Letter,' which I knew the boys would interpret to mean—"

"And in that brochure there was an old photograph of the boys in the arms of their mother and father?"

Mr. Poe nodded.

"And beneath that photo?"

"I inserted a line that could not be misinterpreted."

"And that line was?" Mr. Shakespeare prodded.

"'Stay far away!'"

Shakespeare sighed and shook his head. "Another misprint, Mr. Poe." He sighed. "Ah, who'd imagine two letters could change so much?"

Mr. Poe swallowed hard, worry creeping in again. "So . . . what did the line in the brochure actually say?"

"'Stay for a day.'"

"What!"

"There's nothing we can do."

"I'll write another fortune cookie, and this time—"

"You'll be writing *no more fortune cookies*, Mr. Poe. You're being demoted."

"But the boys are misled!"

Mr. Shakespeare shrugged. "'Fortune brings in some boats that are not steer'd.'"

Shakespeare was quoting Shakespeare again. But that wasn't really what made Mr. Poe angry. He was furious with *himself.* "Your quote is true enough, Mr. Shakespeare. But tell me what happens to boats that are steered in exactly the wrong direction?"

"They crash on the rocks, Mr. Poe."

Mr. Poe stood and pushed past Mr. Shakespeare, heading for the exit.

"Where do you think you're going?" Mr. Shakespeare called.

Mr. Poe didn't answer. He hadn't the slightest idea. Still, there had to be *something* he could do. . . .

TOURIST TRAP

THE next morning at breakfast in the Wagon Wheel Diner, Aunt Judith mashed the pile of strawberries and swirls of whipped cream atop her pancakes into a sweet, chunky mass. Uncle Jack did the same, whistling in approval at the sheer heft of the breakfast before him. In the meantime, Allan and Edgar poked holes into the yolks of their poached eggs, watching the yellow run over the slices of wheat toast before they drenched it all in rivulets of Tabasco sauce, which flowed red as blood over the whole thing. Sometimes watching the Poe family eat was like watching a horror movie.

"How'd you sleep last night, boys?" Aunt Judith asked between bites of strawberry and pancake.

"Sleep was OK," Edgar answered.

"But our waking hours were better," Allan added as he dropped onto the table the brochure they'd discovered in the old book. "Have a look at this."

Aunt Judith picked it up. "It's like the fax in my purse."

Allan shook his head. "This is an older version."

"What's different?" asked Uncle Jack.

"This picture," Edgar said, pointing. "It's us as babies with Mom and Dad."

"Mal and Irma?" Aunt Judith was intrigued.

Uncle Jack took off his glasses in order to get a better look.

Aunt Judith put on her reading glasses and leaned forward, bringing the brochure to within an inch of her face. "What do you know? It *is* Mal and Irma holding you boys!"

Uncle Jack nodded. "They must have come through here when they took one of their crazy vacations."

"Oh, they loved these kinds of wacky roadside attractions," Aunt Judith recalled, smiling. "They'd have surely stopped at that toy-robot museum back in Pennsylvania, or that world's largest ball of human hair in Missouri, just like you two wanted to do. They'd send us postcards. And they'd buy T-shirts and give them away as joke gifts."

"They thought those places were funny," Uncle Jack said.

"They are," the boys agreed, identical grins on their faces.

Uncle Jack chuckled. "You've got their sense of humor."

Aunt Judith looked at her nephews. "Your mom and dad sure loved you two."

Edgar and Allan never knew what to say to things like that—things that somehow, mistakenly, made them feel a little undeserving.

So they said nothing.

Edgar took back the brochure, brushing off a spot of powdered sugar.

"What a lovely coincidence," Aunt Judith said softly. Her expression was a little misty.

The boys didn't bother reminding her what they thought of coincidence. Instead, they slipped the brochure back into the middle of the old book for safekeeping.

"Did you call the professor to tell him we're on our way?" Uncle Jack asked her.

"I tried," she answered as she put her reading glasses back into their case. "But his phone's been disconnected."

Uncle Jack looked confused. "That's strange."

Aunt Judith shrugged. "He probably forgot to pay the

bill. It happens. Besides, when he called us at home he said to just come to his amusement park and we'd be sure to find him."

"He doesn't just work there," Edgar reminded his uncle. "He lives there too."

"What an odd duck," Uncle Jack said.

"Since he's a professor, it's probably more accurate to call him an odd 'doc' rather than an odd 'duck,'" Allan observed.

"Finish your breakfasts," their uncle muttered, and retreated behind his newspaper.

The front page immediately caught the twins' attention—not a news story, but the printed name of the paper itself, which ought to have read

Instead, it was misprinted:

"A typo that actually spells the word 'typos'?" the boys wondered aloud.

"Can you believe such carelessness at a metropolitan newspaper?" Aunt Judith asked.

"What's journalism coming to?" Uncle Jack said, distractedly returning to the sports section.

The boys glanced around the crowded diner. Across the room, a man at the counter was reading from the same morning newspaper, but the front page of *his* copy read KANSAS CITY POST.

No typo.

Just the Poes' newspaper? Surely no mere coincidence.

"'Typos,'" the boys mused. "Not 'typo,' but plural."

"Well, it's off to the Gale Farm," Uncle Jack announced as he refolded the paper, grabbed the check, and began sliding out of the booth. "We're off to see the Wizard, so to speak." He chuckled at his own joke.

Aunt Judith slid out after him. "Won't Roderick be glad to see his boys! It'll be just a couple hours now."

Edgar and Allan still hadn't moved from the booth. Their brains had begun working to process this latest, strangest message:

Typos . . .

"Let's go," Uncle Jack said. "We haven't come all this way just to sit in a diner."

"Boys?" Aunt Judith pressed.

As if in a dream, they rose as one and followed their aunt and uncle out of the restaurant, their brains humming in perfect coordination.

Typos . . .

Then they stopped.

Might some of the recent mysterious messages have contained typos?

"Oh no," they said in unison in the parking lot.

In a flash, they grasped what this latest communiqué meant.

"Wait!" they cried as their aunt and uncle opened the car doors to climb in.

"What is it?" Uncle Jack asked.

The boys processed it, working backward. They substituted letters here and there for every word in every mysterious message they'd received. One ordinary brain would have taken hours to go through all the possibilities—but Edgar and Allan, working together, took mere seconds.

They turned pale when they realized that changing two letters under their old photo in the brochure turned a happy invitation into a dire warning: "Stay far away!" And worse, the "brilliant trip" to the farm was really a brilliant *trap*!

Edgar and Allan looked at each other.

Wasn't this just about picking up the family cat from a kindhearted animal lover? Unless . . .

The boys remembered the poster of the sleeping kitten: "Beware the cat napping." Remove a space and the two words become one: *catnapping*.

Clear as moonlight.

Roderick Usher had been catnapped to lure Edgar and Allan to the Gale Farm, a trap from which they should stay far away!

But who wanted to trap them? And why?

Uncle Jack stood impatiently beside the driver's side door. "Get in, boys. What's wrong with you?"

Danger and deceit . . . That's what was wrong.

But how to explain this to their aunt and uncle?

Even more pressing: what to do about it?

Edgar and Allan knew there was still time to persuade Uncle Jack to turn the car around and safely return home. (Even if he refused, they could always reprogram the car's GPS at the next gas station and be halfway back to Baltimore before Uncle Jack realized he was driving in the wrong direction.) But what then would become of Roderick Usher? The boys would *never* abandon their best friend.

This journey, which had started as a mere retrieval of their cat, was now a full-blown rescue mission, requiring the boys to walk with eyes wide open into some kind of trap.

Hadn't they always wanted to match wits against an opponent more formidable than their school principal?

"Why are you two acting so strange?" Aunt Judith asked with concern.

The boys looked at each other. They knew that the disconnected brains of Uncle Jack and Aunt Judith didn't work as fast as their own. So how to make them understand? Or might their guardians, natural worriers, be better off not knowing? Worry only made things more difficult. Besides, how truly dangerous could a villain be whose lair was a broken-down *Wizard of Oz* amusement park?

"Oh, nothing to fret over," Edgar and Allan said in unison.

The gravel road that led from the highway to the Gale Farm and OZitorium twisted into a dense cornfield, winding among eight-foot-high stalks until soon all that was visible from within the car were walls of corn.

"It's like being in a maze," Edgar said nervously.

"Maize," Aunt Judith remarked, turning and grinning at them. "We're in a maze of maize. You know, M-A-I-Z-E? The Native American word for corn. It's a pun. Do you get it, boys?"

Of course they got it. But that didn't mean they thought it was funny. Still, Aunt Judith had given it her best shot. So they forced crooked smiles.

She beamed.

Soon the stalks thinned, and the road led out of the maize to a dusty lot where a few cars were parked beside two buses.

Uncle Jack pulled in. "All right, boys. Let's find this professor, get your cat, and start back home again."

Edgar and Allan nodded, though they doubted it was going to be quite that simple.

At the emerald-green ticket booth, Uncle Jack grinned widely when a clerk in a funny hat told him the professor had left them free passes. However, the smile faded when the clerk added that the professor was currently "indisposed" and that they should all just "enjoy the park for a couple hours until his schedule cleared."

"After all the miles we've traveled he's too busy to see us?" Uncle Jack said incredulously.

The clerk shrugged, helpless. "Don't worry, sir. He'll track you down in no time. You're his special guests."

The twins didn't like the sound of "track down."

"It'll be OK, Jack," Aunt Judith reassured, patting his arm. "Let's go in."

He turned to her, still put out. "Who does he think we are? His Munchkins?"

"I'm sure it'll be fun," she said, leading him toward the entrance.

The boys weren't sure *what* it was going to be.

Inside the front gate, a cracked cement sidewalk had been painted to look like the Yellow Brick Road. Hedged on either side by tall cornstalks, the path branched in two directions. A signpost pointed one way toward the Authentic Gale Farmhouse, and in the other direction toward the OZitorium.

There were very few other tourists around.

And oddly—particularly for a sunny Saturday—there were no children.

Instead, they were either old folks wearing wide-brimmed sun hats or middle-aged couples dressed in embarrassing colors (or worse, in husband-wife matching outfits). An amusement park with no kids? The boys wondered if this was a sign of danger or just characteristic of *any* crummy roadside attraction.

"This is a strange place for a professor to call home," Aunt Judith observed.

"Not if he's a strange professor," said Edgar, his tone a bit suspicious.

"Or a professor of the strange," Allan added.

Uncle Jack gave the boys a funny look.

"Maybe he's in the farmhouse," their aunt suggested reasonably.

Uncle Jack nodded and started in that direction.

The other three Poes followed.

They rounded a corner and arrived at the crest of the hill.

From there, they could see the farm, which looked like *any* abandoned, broken-down, century-old place, only worse. The barn consisted of a small forest's worth of rotting wood piled haphazardly within the boundaries of a barely recognizable barn-shaped frame; the pigpens were empty; the water tower leaked; and the farmhouse was nothing more than a collapsed pile of splintered wood, roof shingles, and twisted metal bed frames and stovepipes. In short, the house looked exactly like what it claimed to be: a small wooden structure that had been lifted off its foundations and into the air by a tornado and then dropped from a great height. *Crash!* It was hardly a house at all anymore.

A sign beside the wreckage read:

```
┌─────────────────────────────────┐
│                                 │
│    AUTHENTIC FORMER HOME        │
│      OF DOROTHY GALE            │
│                                 │
└─────────────────────────────────┘
```

"That's all there is to it?" Aunt Judith said.

Uncle Jack shook his head, disgruntled. "The professor must be at the OZitorium, whatever *that* is."

The boys kept their eyes open for anything unusual or threatening as they retraced their steps and then took the other path, passing a souvenir stand that sold T-shirts, DVDs of *The Wizard of Oz*, paperback editions of the Oz books, snow globes, Toto dog leashes, and "authentic" Dorothy Gale sunglasses and cell-phone cases. They continued around a bend until they came to the OZitorium, which was just an ordinary-looking auditorium. A murmur of voices from inside resolved itself into music and singing as the Poe family drew nearer.

"*We're off to see the Wizard, the Wonderful Wizard of Oz . . .*"

Aunt Judith smiled. "Oh, I do love a live show."

A sign above the entrance to the OZitorium read:

At the entrance, the Poes were stopped by an attendant dressed like an old-time movie usher. He was as
round as he was tall and wore a walkie-talkie holstered
on his hip.

"Sorry," he told them. "No one's allowed inside after
the show begins. Come back at three thirty. Until then,
you can tour the authentic Gale Farm."

"We already did," Aunt Judith said.

"It took about two seconds," Uncle Jack added
dryly.

"Well, I don't make the policy," the attendant said,
looking past them as if on guard against nonexistent
battalions of gate crashers. "Now, why don't you all just
move along?"

"Look, we're not actually here for the show," Uncle
Jack said. "We're here to see the professor."

"Yes, he found the boys' lost cat," Aunt Judith added.

The security guard's eyes widened. He moved away from them, turned his back, and whispered into the walkie-talkie. The boys couldn't really hear what he said, but they caught this much: "Poe twins."

They didn't wait around for more.

By the time the security guard turned back to the Poe family, saying, "It seems we've made special arrangements for you folks," the boys had disappeared. He looked around, worried. "Hey, where'd they go?"

Uncle Jack and Aunt Judith had no idea.

WHAT THE POE TWINS DID NOT KNOW . . .

From: Archer@The-poes.net
Sent: Sat, Nov 19, 11:10 am
To: perry@The-poes.net
Subject: Monkey Business

Professor Perry,

All is ready. As planned, the park is populated today only by our invited guests, the local Etiquette Society. This will ensure that the Poe brats stumble upon no natural allies. In further accordance with your brilliant plans, security will move in on the twins and their guardians at the conclusion of the play.

If it's all right with you, sir, I would like to rejoin the cast today, in my old role, as a way of commemorating this day and your historic triumph.

Admiringly,
Ian Archer

MONKEYS

ALLAN and Edgar knew what they had to do: find and recover Roderick Usher, then rejoin their aunt and uncle and get out of there, all the while avoiding whatever nefarious plot the professor had in mind for them. And they had to do it quickly, as they suspected their nemesis already knew they were here.

So they raced away from the entrance to the OZitorium and toward the back of the building to make a plan in private.

As they rounded the corner it was not solitude they discovered but a long trailer that served as a dressing room for the musical's cast members. The place buzzed with activity as a dozen little men and women scurried about, some costumed as Munchkins, others as flying monkeys. The boys looked at each other—in other circumstances, this might be fun. Today was serious business.

Just then, a quartet of private security guards, all more formidable-looking than the usher at the front entrance, emerged from around the far corner, their handcuffs clattering on their belts, their walkie-talkies held at the ready.

There was no place for the boys to hide, and running away would only draw attention—so, lightning-fast, they infiltrated a nearby group of female Munchkins who were doing ballet exercises to loosen up before going onstage. Their backs to the guards, the boys imitated the ladies. They were glad none of their classmates was there to see them do the daintiest of the stretches, but the ruse worked. The security guards continued past.

Clearly, there was no time to waste.

The first thing the boys needed was a disguise.

They entered the trailer's dressing room. "Where are the costumes, miss?" Edgar politely asked a Munchkin princess.

"Munchkin costume or flying monkey costume?" she inquired in a high-pitched voice.

"Flying monkeys, of course," the boys answered.

"Over there," she said, pointing to a rack against one wall.

A few minutes later, in furry costumes and head-pieces, Edgar and Allan were identical to those around them, just as they ordinarily were to each other.

Edgar   Allan   Others

"Attention! Flying monkeys, we're onstage in five minutes," called their leader, who was differentiated from the other monkeys by a blue ribbon on his uniform. "Let's go."

His voice sounded familiar, though the twins couldn't quite place it. The other flying monkeys shuffled into the center of the room. Edgar and Allan took the opportunity to slowly drift toward the back.

"This is a very special day for the professor, so let's put on a great show," Flying Monkey Number One said to his underlings as they lined up in single file. "Egad, you're a motley bunch!" he added.

Egad?

The boys' stomachs lurched. Nobody used that word anymore. That is, no one but the mysterious little man from the principal's office—the hair plucker, Mr. Archer. *That's* why his voice sounded familiar! So this *did* stretch all the way back to Baltimore.

Or might it go back even further than that?

Unnoticed, Edgar and Allan continued backing away from the group and then slipped behind a costume rack. From there, they watched the simian squadron follow Number One/Mr. Archer out of the dressing room.

As a precaution, the boys waited two minutes.

Stillness, silence . . .

Emerging from behind the rack, they adjusted the monkey headpieces, lining up the eye holes to see out, and crossed the room to the door. Yes, the costumes were good. But was their posture monkeylike enough to blend in with the others?

No.

So Edgar hunched his shoulders and bent forward at

the waist, allowing his arms to dangle. Allan imitated him, then bent his knees and turned his feet outward to add a convincing spring to his step. Edgar did the same.

Yes, better.

Allan opened the door. Outside, this was what they spied:

A few aged park visitors mingled harmlessly beside a cotton candy cart being operated by a bored teenage girl in an ill-fitting Glinda the Good costume. Near the entrance to the restrooms stood a pair of reed-thin ladies and their pot-bellied husbands, all talking distractedly on smartphones. Finally, beside an overfull trash can near the back entrance to the OZitorium, a trio of crows pecked at spilled popcorn.

There was no one else around—no flying monkeys, no Munchkins, and, most important, no security guards.

Relieved, Edgar turned to Allan, looking him up and down. "You know," he said, "just because you look like a monkey, you don't have to smell like one too."

Allan smirked, though of course the headpiece hid his expression. "Very funny," he muttered sarcastically (he'd thought of the identical joke just a moment before). "I guess it takes one to smell one."

Now Edgar smirked too.

(Actually, the boys couldn't smell anything except the musty odor of fake fur and a subtle hint of the Tabasco sauce they'd accidentally dripped on their shirts that morning at breakfast.)

"What we need," Edgar observed, "is not the smell of monkeys but to have a monkey's *sense* of smell."

"Yeah, that way we could sniff our way to wherever the professor is holding Roderick Usher."

"I guess we'll have to use our brains instead," Allan said.

The boys put their minds to work.

Within seconds, the air inside their monkey head-pieces heated up by at least three or four degrees.

After a moment, they had it figured out.

"Where's the best place to hide valuables?" Edgar asked, knowing the answer.

"In a pile of junk," said Allan.

"And what's the biggest pile of junk on the premises?"

There was little doubt. "The Dorothy Gale farm-house and barn."

"Exactly!"

"I'll look for a secret entrance in the house," Allan volunteered.

"I'll take the barn."

And the boys were off, shuffling and skipping with arms dangling, retracing their steps along the painted yellow path like a pair of slightly drunk primates.

By this point, most of the tourists (including Uncle Jack and Aunt Judith) were seated in the OZitorium watching the live musical production of the *Wizard of Oz*. So when Edgar and Allan arrived back at the "authentic" Gale family farm buildings, they encountered only a few disinterested stragglers who assumed the costumed boys were park employees.

The furry pair jumped over the picket fence that separated the exhibit from the pathway.

Allan started exploring the ruins of the farmhouse.

Edgar began combing through the massive woodpile that had once been the barn.

What a bunch of junk! the two thought as they sorted through splintery boards and rusted sheet metal. The minutes ticked by. . . .

Allan was the first to find something of interest.

In the rubble of the farmhouse, he spotted an old-fashioned toilet and overhead water tank, the sort used a hundred years ago. This stopped him. Wouldn't such

a modest old farmhouse have relied on an outhouse instead of indoor plumbing? Adding to his suspicions was the fact that there were no twisted, rusted pipes anywhere near the toilet. Intrigued, he examined the antique tank, which was at about eye level.

He pulled the chain to flush it.

As there were no pipes, there was no actual flush, no flow of water. Instead, there was an unexpected metallic grinding nearby . . . and what had appeared to be an eight-foot-square section of collapsed roof proved to be a secret door that slid open to reveal a hidden room.

Always remember to flush, Allan thought.

From atop the nearby junk pile that had been the barn, Edgar watched his brother slip into the newly revealed room. "Clever monkey," he murmured.

Then he returned his attention to his own heap of planks and rusted hardware, looking for anything unusual that might serve as a key to a hidden room there, too. But he spied only a jumble of weathered, rotted hickory and pine. Nothing as obvious as an unplumbed toilet.

Then he noticed a single weathered plank of oak, indistinguishable from the hickory and pine to all but the most experienced carpenters or arborists. Edgar was no carpenter, but fortunately he had a passing interest in arboriculture.

He went to the incongruous plank and pressed his furry foot on it.

A loud *crack!*

And then . . . you guessed it.

A nearby section of rubble slid aside to reveal a secret room there as well.

These were no ordinary piles of junk.

And we're no ordinary monkeys, Edgar thought before disappearing into the dark space.

WHAT THE POE TWINS DID NOT KNOW . . .

A LETTER DELIVERED TO THE AUTHENTIC GALE FARM
AND OZITORIUM TWO DAYS BEFORE:

IGER COFFIN MAKERS
Serving discreet customers since 1845

Dear Professor,

Tonight, we will be making the midnight
delivery of one child-size coffin, as scheduled.
Your business is important to us and we take
pride in offering our clients the best prices.

Sincerely,

Markus Iger, Esq.

P.S. We are sorry to report that we no longer
offer discounts for child-size coffins.

STAGE FRIGHT

ALLAN looked through the doorway and into the small secret chamber he'd uncovered by flushing the old toilet in the rubble of the Gale house. The walls were painted a crisp white, and the floor was tiled in a checkerboard pattern of black and red. At the center of the room, on a small metal table, was an old-fashioned desktop computer, its heavy, glowing monitor as deep as it was wide. Otherwise the place was empty—no chair, no lighting fixtures, no pictures on the walls, nothing.

As secret lairs go, this one was more like a basement than a Bat Cave.

Allan stepped inside, glancing back at the door, hoping it wouldn't slam shut behind him (as he knew secret doors had a tendency to do). He moved toward the computer, confident that his hacking skills would be useful.

But the computer was so old, slow, and weak that even Allan was unable to make it do what he wanted. Dating from the early nineties, it offered little more networking options than a portable TV set. Allan groaned at the cruel irony of being defeated not by high tech but by low tech. Was this professor some sort of outmoded fool? Or was he an unexpectedly clever adversary?

So Edgar did the only thing he could do: he watched the screen.

It showed a live black-and-white image of the front entrance to the Gale Farm and OZitorium. Not much happening there. If all this was just an ordinary security camera setup, then why hide it in a secret room?

After a few seconds, the image shifted to a view from another camera—this time a shot of the parking lot. Cars, buses, nothing of note. . . . Next, the OZitorium, outside of which a pair of burly security guards paced. Allan was about to turn away when the next image caught his attention.

It was the exterior of the Poe family house back in Baltimore.

"Our *house*?"

Next, the screen switched to a live, hidden-camera shot of the Poe family's backyard.

"What?" This was creepy.

And last, a feed from behind the heating grate of the twins' own bedroom!

Who's been spying on us? Allan wondered.

Of course, he knew the answer. What he didn't know was why. Or how. Had that repairman who'd rewired their house last year been working secretly for the professor? Or the plumber who'd put in the new upstairs bathroom over the summer? Or the carpet layers who'd replaced the old shag in the basement after the boys' Halloween prank ruined it? Or someone else from the crew who'd built Aunt Judith's classroom? Had one of them secretly installed cameras?

Meantime, Edgar had entered the secret room he'd uncovered in the ruins of the barn. This room was outfitted with sufficient survival supplies to sustain a man for months—for example, a full pantry of canned food and bottled water. In the corner was a toilet. Against one wall was a cot and against another was a shelf of books. Edgar examined the titles of the books, all of which were about either quantum physics or the lives of infamous men—Attila the Hun, Vlad the Impaler, Ivan the Terrible.

What sort of man builds himself such a hideout?

A madman, Edgar thought.

Then he noticed a scrawled note on the edge of the bookshelf, perhaps forgotten by its distracted author.

> *NOTE TO STAFF:*
> *The name of my new black cat—who has a white figure 8 on his chest—is Asparagus. He's mine, so hands off!*

Edgar grabbed the note and raced from the room.

Allan was waiting for him outside.

Neither boy had to explain to the other what he'd found, because both already knew.

"How creepy is that video stuff?" Allan said.

Edgar agreed. "And why would he rename our cat 'Asparagus'?"

"Sounds familiar."

"Isn't it from a poem?" Edgar asked.

The air inside the boys' headpieces once again grew warmer as their minds began to whir.

"Of course! It's from T. S. Eliot's *Old Possum's Book of Practical Cats*!" Allan exclaimed.

Naturally, the twins considered Eliot an inferior poet to their great-great-great-great granduncle; nonetheless, they were familiar with his light verse.

"And in the poem, Asparagus the cat is also known as—"

"Gus the theatre cat!" Allan finished.

"Looks like it's showtime."

Allan nodded his furry head. "Handy that we're already in our costumes."

Having slipped unnoticed through the backstage door of the OZitorium, Edgar and Allan mixed with the other flying monkeys, all of whom were gathered in the wings awaiting their next cue. The boys looked out onto the stage.

A bank of spotlights cast sections in different colors: emerald green for the glittering city of Oz; a mysterious gray with hints of purple and blue where the dark forest loomed; stark, silvery white with heavy shadows for the Wicked Witch's castle. Then the scene went dark and the boys could see into the audience, where maybe a hundred tourists, almost all of them over age sixty, sat on folding chairs.

Flying Monkey Number One—aka Mr. Archer—whispered to his charges, "OK, everybody, time to hook up."

Hook up? Edgar and Allan looked around, confused.

The other flying monkeys all grabbed at ropes that hung from the distant rafters, fastening the hooks at the ends onto a small loop at the back of their costumes.

Edgar and Allan were not inclined to hook themselves onto anything. It seemed too much like being tied up. No way.

"You're on, everybody. Go, go!"

And just like that Allan and Edgar were swept onstage and into the re-lit spotlights with their flying monkey companions. The boys hesitated at center stage, looking around; after a moment, they began doing as the other monkeys did, hopping in tiny circles. No sense drawing attention to themselves. . . .

Meantime, the Wicked Witch, whose thick stage makeup was the color of lime Jell-O, gazed into a giant crystal ball and shrieked: "Bring me that girl and her dog!" Her cackling filled the auditorium.

The boys looked out beyond the stage, hoping to catch sight of their aunt and uncle, but against the glare of the spotlights they couldn't pick them out. However, they noted that all the exits to the OZitorium were now guarded by security.

The Wicked Witch looked up from her crystal ball as Edgar, Allan, and the other flying monkeys hopped around her. Her eyes blazed with dramatized malice as she turned to her squadron of furry henchmen. "Now fly! Fly!" she cried.

At her cue, the flying monkeys—all but two, of course—rose off the stage floor, pulled toward the rafters by the ropes hooked to their backs. One foot above the ground, then two, five, eight . . . The boys looked up as a matrix of pulleys, rotating arms, and levers pulled their furry compatriots high into the air and then began to swing them in widening arcs. Some of the monkeys even glided out over the audience.

Edgar and Allan couldn't help but be a little envious.

The Wicked Witch turned angrily to the two grounded monkeys at her side. "What's wrong with you two?" she whispered, her non-actress voice betraying an un-witchlike Brooklyn accent. "Get your butts up in the air," she hissed. "The professor's in the house today. Get it right."

The professor was in the audience?

"Where is he?" the boys hissed back.

"Where he always is," she answered. Huffily, she turned back to the audience, ad-libbing: "I keep these two smelly apes with me as my personal bodyguards."

Ordinarily, the boys would have come back with a

cutting remark of their own—perhaps something about *her* being the smelly one, seeing as witches who are melted by water must never bathe or shower—but they didn't want to call attention to themselves, not even for a laugh.

Meantime, the other winged monkeys swung and swooped about the stage, distracting the audience. The boys backed away from the witch, crossing their furry fingers in hopes that the spotlight wouldn't follow them. To their relief, they made it into the shadows upstage, unnoticed.

But what now?

They still needed to find Roderick Usher, rejoin their aunt and uncle, and then escape without Mr. Archer catching them. But was Mr. Archer really their most fearsome threat? The boys suspected it was actually the unseen professor who was pulling the strings.

The boys were right.

However, at that moment the professor was pulling a rope, not a string. A rope that was connected to one of the two dozen trapdoors on the stage—specifically, the door upon which the boys now stood.

For a moment, Edgar and Allan felt weightless.

Before they could say "Isaac Newton," they plummeted into darkness.

The fall through the trapdoor—from the brightly lit stage of the OZitorium to the darkness beneath—was only twelve feet, but it felt farther to Edgar and Allan. Fortunately, they landed in a heap atop a pile of dusty stage curtains that was thick enough to spare them broken heads (though not thick enough to prevent them from seeing stars). By the time their vision cleared, the trapdoor had snapped shut. The ruckus of the play above was audible now only as a dim rattle, as if it were miles away.

"Hello, boys," came a raspy voice.

A gas lantern flared in a corner of the room.

In the flickering light, the boys could make out a man about their uncle's age seated in an electric wheelchair. Clamped to the arm of the chair was a small video monitor. Beside him was a low wooden panel with a dozen foot-long handles connected to a matrix of ropes that radiated up to the stage floor and farther up into the invisible rafters of the theater.

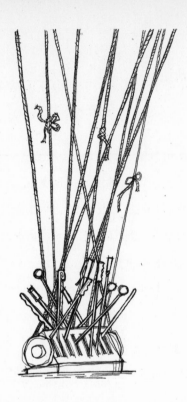

Like a spider at the center of a web, he sat in complete control.

"Glad you could drop in," he said.

❧☠❧

WHAT THE POE TWINS DID NOT KNOW...

DRAFT OF UNMAILED CORRESPONDENCE,
NOT YET SET IN CODE

From the Desk of
PROFESSOR S. PANGBORN PERRY, PhD

Mother (Prisoner #89372),

Your latest letter was quite disappointing to me. Have you acquired no wisdom in your eighty-seven years of life? Why would I want to change? Especially now, the very day that I'm to achieve my destiny. Don't you know how long and patiently I've waited for those two brats to become old enough that they could be of service to me? Since they were infants! And now you, a convicted felon, choose to question my character?

Oh well, Mother, soon enough you'll understand why I planted that evidence years ago so you'd go to prison instead of me. And you'll finally admit that your freedom has been a small sacrifice for the greatness I'm about to achieve.

Believe me, when I've gained world domination I will make the cops who've been looking for me all this time regret their career choice.

Sincerely,
Your Son

UNDERWORLD

THE man had bushy eyebrows and slicked-back white hair. At first glance he looked very like his namesake, Professor Marvel from the *Wizard of Oz* movie. Amid the cloud of dust particles raised by the boys' fall, his appearance wavered and shimmered, almost ghostlike. Something black moved in his lap.

Edgar clambered to his feet. "Roderick—"

"Usher!" Allan finished, right beside him.

The twins' cat attempted to leap toward them but was jerked back by a leash the professor held in one fist.

"Stay with me, Asparagus," the professor hissed.

Enraged, Edgar and Allan started toward the brute but stopped when he showed them the shiny silver pistol in his other hand.

"Take off those ridiculous masks so I can see your faces, Edgar and Allan Poe."

They followed his order. "How'd you know who we were?"

He kept the gun on them. "You were the only two monkeys on that stage whose movements were perfectly coordinated with one another. *Mirror images*, you might say. Also, you were the only two monkeys not hooked into my rope system."

Drat, the boys thought. Even with two minds working as one it was impossible to cover every possibility.

"Oh, your disguises may have outfoxed my assistant," he continued, his mouth twisting as he spoke. "Of course, that's not saying much. Mr. Archer is loyal, but he possesses a merely *ordinary* intellect. He is no match for you two. Fortunately, I was monitoring everything, so your costumed mischief has done no harm, and you're still right where I wanted you all along."

"What do you want with us?" Allan asked, mopping his brow with one furry hand.

The professor took a deep breath. "Oh, we'll get to that soon enough, but first allow me to introduce myself."

"We know who you are," Edgar said.

"You're Professor Marvel," Allan said.

The man snorted. "Actually, my real name is Professor S. Pangborn Perry, PhD, P.O.E.S."

The twins knew a PhD was the highest academic degree granted by universities, but as for the rest of his credentials—they didn't think Professor Perry was a member of the Parents of Exceptional Students. "What's the P-O-E-S stand for?" they asked.

"Physicist of Extreme Science," he answered.

"'Extreme science'?"

"Have you boys heard of 'extreme sports'?"

"Like skateboarding off a ten-story ramp or snow-boarding off a cliff?"

"Exactly," answered the professor. "That's how I approach my scientific research."

"So why 'Professor Marvel'?" Allan asked.

"That's a cover name I chose years ago, well suited both to this place and to my ambitious genius."

"You seem more like a Professor Moriarty," Edgar observed, referring to the master criminal in the Sherlock Holmes stories.

The professor made a face, as if he'd been exposed to a

bad smell. "You insult me. Moriarty was a minor-leaguer. One only has to study the Oz story, boys." He waved the gun casually as he spoke, still clutching Roderick Usher close to him with his other hand. "Professor Marvel, also known as the Wizard, is the greatest nefarious genius ever portrayed in the movies. Think about it. The Wicked Witch is merely a pathetic, grieving wretch who lives in a drafty castle with mutant monkeys. Meantime, Professor Marvel becomes dictator of the entire land of Oz, relaxing in luxury in a city made of *emeralds*. When threatened, he sends Dorothy and her friends to assassinate his only rival, the witch. Not a very *nice* guy . . . but powerful. Until he goes soft at the end of the story. That's where we differ."

"This place isn't exactly made of emeralds," Allan observed.

"Not to mention your out-of-date electronics," added Edgar.

The professor frowned. "Don't underestimate my little roadside attraction, boys. It has not only allowed me to become a more refined version of my own boyhood hero, but it has also served me well as a hideout from the authorities."

"Why are the authorities looking for you?"

"They suspect I was involved in a murder. Or two. Or more."

"Were you?"

"Ah, boys . . ." He grinned again. His teeth were yellow—did he never brush? "The past is past. Why don't we just leave it that way? Particularly since the future is so bright. For me, at least."

Edgar and Allan began to inch apart, a classic evasive maneuver.

"Stop!" the professor shouted, dumping Roderick Usher from his lap so he could use both hands for better aim.

The boys made eye contact with Roderick, directing him with their gaze toward a pile of dusty props and the safety of darkness. After a moment, Roderick took cover, trailing his leash after him. In the shadows, only his glowing eyes were visible.

"Move apart another inch and I'll fire," the professor said, calm again.

The boys stopped.

"Your mother and father never knew what they had with you two," he said almost regretfully.

"You knew them?" Edgar asked.

"Yes, but they never truly knew *me*." His sinister expression lightened. "You may be interested to know that your mother and father actually brought you boys to this place when you were babies."

"We know. We've seen a picture."

The professor brushed aside their words. "Oh, the ridiculous attractions your folks dragged me through as I shadowed you all on that trip. The World's Largest Sassafras Tree in Owensboro, Kentucky. The World's Largest Catsup Bottle in Collinsville, Illinois. The Pencil Sharpener Museum in Logan, Ohio. But I have to admit I'd never have stumbled across this place otherwise. And years later, when I needed a hideout, I returned here, to my own private Oz, to rule. The owner didn't want to sell it to me at first. But it didn't take me long to change his mind . . . may he rest in peace."

The boys gulped, their Adam's apples moving up and down in perfect synchronization. "You were interested in us even as babies?"

"Oh, I had you two pegged early."

"How?"

He sighed. "Look, when it comes to twins there are three kinds: fraternal, identical, and . . . you."

The boys already knew they were unusual. "So what?"

He puffed up his chest and raised his voice, as if addressing a crowded lecture hall rather than a dusty, below-stage basement. "Recent experiments in quantum physics confirm a strange phenomenon called 'quantum entanglement.' This phenomenon—"

"Yeah, yeah, we know about it," the boys interrupted in unison. "Einstein called it 'spooky action at a distance.'"

"Very good," the professor said, impressed. "But Einstein lacked the courage to go all the way. Only *I* have dared to imagine what might occur if the two joined objects were not just particles but human beings! Two bodies, two locations, but *one shared mind* . . ."

The twins didn't like where this was going.

"Quantum entanglement applies only to subatomic particles, not people," Allan said.

"Except in the rarest of cases," the professor countered.

"The odds against such a thing would be trillions to one," Edgar observed.

The professor nodded. "And that's why you two boys are so valuable. That's why you *must* be put to scientific use. That's why I must have you."

Allan and Edgar couldn't help but be impressed by the boldness of the professor's theory—of course, his character and motives were an entirely different matter.

"If we're so valuable, why would you want to shoot us?"

"Oh, I plan on shooting only one of you." The professor's chair wheeled closer. "Imagine one of you dead, relocated to the 'next world.' Now imagine the other my lifelong prisoner, still receiving and transmitting communications to and from his deceased brother, to and from the 'great beyond,' the 'hereafter,' 'Heaven,' 'the underworld,' whatever you want to call it. Yes, a direct line to the land of the dead. Imagine what one could do with the knowledge. Rule the world! Rule *both* worlds!"

The boys' hearts began to race.

Pushing a button on the arm of his chair, the professor activated the overhead lights. The fluorescence burned for a moment in the boys' eyes. But now they could see the whole room. It was crowded with stage props, some of which seemed to have nothing to do with *The Wizard of Oz*. An old-fashioned, wind-up phonograph sat atop a pirate's treasure chest beside a six-foot-tall hat rack and a scattering of tables, chairs, and accessories.

They didn't actually notice the boy-sized coffin standing upright against a far wall until the professor pointed it out to them.

"That coffin's not a theatrical prop," he said. "It's real. It has fine brass hinges and a lovely satin lining. And it's for one of you."

The boys had to admit: it *was* a nice coffin.

Still, neither was ready to claim it for his own.

"You can't shoot us," Edgar said confidently. "The people outside will hear the shot and come running."

The professor shook his head and smiled again. "This is a well-built theater. We're soundproofed down here."

Edgar looked at Allan. Allan looked at Edgar.

It didn't look good.

The professor aimed his gun first at one boy, then the other. "Let's see," he mused. "Which will it be? I suppose in the end it doesn't matter."

Desperate, the boys glanced up to the ceiling, which was actually the underside of the stage. There hung the web of ropes, pulleys, heavy sandbags, and counter-weights that operated the trapdoors in the stage and controlled the monkeys' flying mechanisms high up in the theater's invisible rafters. The twin minds worked at lightning speed: What if the *right* rope was to break, particularly now that the professor had wheeled himself directly beneath one of the heavy counterweights?

"Would one of you like to volunteer for the 'next world'?" the professor taunted, turning his gun on Edgar, then Allan, and then back again. "Or shall *I* decide?"

The boys said nothing.

Instead, they began whistling "Ring Around the Rosy."

Roderick poked his head out from behind the props, out of the professor's line of vision. He had cleverly slipped his collar and leash.

The man smiled. "Ah, whistling in the face of death. I give you both points for style, boys."

Being a well-trained cat, Roderick leaped to the taut web of ropes beneath the stage, directly above the professor.

Now all the twins needed to do was stall for time.

"We have one last request," they said hurriedly, before the professor could pull the trigger.

"Yes?"

"Before you send one of us into the 'next world,' will you tell us how you became such a distinguished and unmatched genius?"

The professor straightened in his wheelchair, surprised. "That's an outstanding question. I'm glad you boys aren't taking this dying stuff too personally."

"And can you start from the beginning?" Allan asked.

"Oh, I'm afraid there isn't time for that," the professor said. "But since you asked, I will share a few insights about my journey, my genius, myself."

The boys encouraged him to continue.

Roderick Usher started on his work in the rafters, fraying, fraying, fraying . . .

His claws were sharp, his paws fast.

But would they be fast enough?

When the professor's egotistical ramblings began to wrap up, the twins pressed for more.

"When did you first realize you were a genius?" Edgar asked.

With ironic timing, the heavy counterweight directly above the professor snapped loose from the newly frayed rope and came down on his head just as he said, "My genius came upon me suddenly, like a bolt of lightning out of the sky—"

Bam!

He tipped in a heap out of his wheelchair to the ground, unconscious.

"Nice work, Roderick!" the twins cheered.

The cat leaped down from the rafters and wove a figure eight around their legs.

Still, not all was well.

Above them, they heard crashes, clanks, and thuds. The rope that Roderick Usher had loosed held more than just one counterweight—it was part of the web that controlled all the trapdoors in the stage. Suddenly, long lengths of rope whipped through the pulleys, snapping at the air like angry serpents, and counterweights began to fall all around the boys, exploding fragments of cement wherever they landed.

And making matters worse . . .

The trapdoors in the stage *all* fell open at once.

Whatever props or scenery the trapdoors supported plunged down, crashing all around the boys. The half-ton brass machine used to simulate the Wizard of Oz in his grandiose, flame-breathing disguise fell just inches from where they stood.

Crash!

Next, band instruments plummeted from the stage, including the drum kit and piano.

Clang! Boom!

And the musicians who played the instruments.

Ouch!

Seconds later, the Wicked Witch, Dorothy, the Scarecrow, and the other actors fell from above as if they'd actually been dropped by a tornado.

The boys could only jump out of the way.

But where were the dangerous Mr. Archer and the other flying monkeys?

Looking up through the open trapdoors, Edgar and Allan saw why no monkeys had fallen into the basement—they'd all been jerked upward to the top of the theater, where their ropes tangled with the rafters. There they dangled helplessly, thirty feet up, in a single ball of kicking fur.

The panicked audience of the OZitorium couldn't see

the mayhem taking place above and below the stage, but they heard it. There was a mad rush for the exits, everyone pushing and shoving despite their Etiquette Society training.

Who'd have thought so much could come from the untying of one rope?

Roderick Usher leaped into Edgar's arms and mewed at the boys.

"Let's get out of here," Allan said.

"Over there!" Edgar indicated a metal stairwell that led up to a door marked Exit.

"What about that dried-up old spider?" Allan asked, pointing to the professor, who remained unconscious beside his tipped wheelchair. "Should we tie him up?"

"He's not going anywhere. We'll tell the cops where to find him."

They raced up the metal stairs and pushed on the door, hoping it wasn't locked.

It flew open.

The three tumbled into the sunlight, safe.

WHAT THE POE TWINS DID NOT KNOW . . .

TEXT MESSAGE FROM THE CELL PHONE OF IAN ARCHER TO THE CELL PHONE OF PROFESSOR S. PANGBORN PERRY (AKA PROFESSOR MARVEL), SENT WHILE ARCHER DANGLED FROM THE CEILING OF THE OZITORIUM:

> Where are you, sir? Police everywhere! I'll say nothing to them, but I'm counting on you to get me out of this. Fast.

SECOND TEXT MESSAGE FROM THE CELL PHONE OF IAN ARCHER TO THE CELL PHONE OF PROFESSOR S. PANGBORN PERRY, SENT FOURTEEN MINUTES AFTER THE FIRST MESSAGE:

> Still no response. Curse you, Professor! If you don't get me out of this fix in 48 hours I swear I'll start singing. Yup, I'll tell the cops all about the Poe twins' parents, how their "accident" was no accident.

NO FURTHER TEXT MESSAGES TO OR FROM THE CELL PHONES OF IAN ARCHER AND PROFESSOR S. PANGBORN PERRY.

STARS

THE next day at the press conference, when Edgar and Allan emerged with their aunt and uncle through the wide double doors of the county courthouse, hundreds of cameras flashed in their direction. To the boys, it appeared to be a whole galaxy of tiny, exploding stars. Dozens of shouted questions arose from the crowd of reporters, photographers, television cameramen, and sound engineers who pushed and jockeyed at the foot of the old building's wide staircase for the best view of the boys.

"Look at that mob," Allan whispered to his brother.

Edgar nodded. "If any group of kids ever acted this out-of-control they'd probably get detention for life."

The camera flashes continued and the shouted questions came so fast and furious that even with two brains operating in perfect coordination, the Poe boys could make little sense of it. The mayor, who looked like the host of Aunt Judith's favorite TV game show, smiled reassuringly and led the family to a podium that had been set up at the top of the stairs beneath a banner that read:

WELCOME, POES!!!

Edgar and Allan knew for certain that this time the welcome wasn't for Parents of Exemplary Students—and most certainly not for Physicists of Extreme Science.

The mayor commanded the podium. He tapped the microphone. The boys half expected him to introduce them as the "daily double." Disappointingly, he merely delivered a boring speech.

"It is my distinct pleasure," he said, in a voice that had little game-show excitement in it, "to welcome you distinguished ladies and gentlemen of the media to our lovely town and to assure you that we will make your stay with us . . ."

To the boys it sounded like "Blah, blah, blah."

Eventually, the mayor got around to the facts: "These two boys, working entirely on their own, identified, caught, and detained two dangerous criminals, one of whom they rendered unconscious and the other of whom they tied up for the police."

"How did you boys track 'em down?" a reporter shouted.

"How'd you figure it out, Edgar and Allan?" another asked.

"Did you ever fear for your safety?" a third reporter called.

The mayor held up his hand to silence the reporters, and continued with his statement: "The arrest of Mr. Ian Archer, who is high on the FBI's Most Wanted List, represents an important victory for law enforcement. Trust me, ladies and gentlemen of the press, Batman himself couldn't have delivered a criminal to us in a neater package."

Hands shot up among the members of the press and dozens more questions were shouted, but the mayor ignored them and continued:

"But even *more* significantly, these boys captured Professor S. Pangborn Perry, a wanted felon who has been living in these parts for seven years under the name of 'Professor Marvel.'"

"Have you boys solved crimes before?" a reporter interrupted.

"What brought you to Kansas?" another called.

"Would you boys be willing to do an interview for the local news?"

Again, the mayor held up his hand. "Please! Ladies and gentlemen . . ."

Reluctantly, the press corps quieted.

"Mr. Archer, arrested while disguised as a winged monkey, is currently in police custody," the mayor continued. "Meantime, Professor Perry, who received a severe blow to the head, remains unconscious in a local hospital where he is under twenty-four-hour police guard. That these boys traced these criminals to our town, when even the FBI could not do so, speaks to their amazing deductive powers."

Next, the rotund police chief, dressed in a uniform clanking with medals, walked up to the podium. He cleared his throat. "It's my honor to present to these boys the Kansas Commissioner's Medal, the highest honor given to private citizens for contributions to crime-fighting."

Amid a furious clatter of cameras, the chief pinned a twin set of shiny medals on Allan and Edgar.

"Your mother and father would be very proud of you," Uncle Jack whispered to the boys.

"As *we're* proud," Aunt Judith added.

Hearing these words felt good to the boys—even better than receiving medals.

The roar of questions only got louder and more out of hand when the twins started toward the microphone.

"How'd you boys figure it out?"

"What were the clues you followed?"

"How'd the two of you infiltrate the professor's lair?"

Edgar and Allan had decided it was too risky to tell the press the whole truth—some other lunatic might come after them if the professor's "quantum entanglement" theory went public.

Edgar stepped up to the mike, straining on tiptoe to reach it. "First, you all should know that we're the great-great-great-great grandnephews of the author Edgar Allan Poe. So we start with a bit of an advantage in the imagination department." He pointed to the journalists. "Go ahead, write that down."

"Can you be more specific?" they asked.

Allan joined his brother, rising to his tiptoes, too. "Sorry, but we captured these criminals using an ingenious thought process that would be impossible for most of you to follow."

Edgar raised his eyebrows. "Is anyone here the great-great-great-great grandnephew or grandniece of, say, Sherlock Holmes?"

No one raised a hand.

"In that case," Allan said, "let's just leave it at this: we solved the crime and you didn't."

"Thank you for your attention, ladies and gentlemen," Edgar said.

"Wait!" a reporter shouted. "What are your plans for the future?"

The boys looked at each other. "For now, we're just planning to spend time with our friend Roderick Usher."

"Roderick who?" the reporters shouted.

"Our cat."

"Can we get his picture too?"

The boys shook their heads no. "He's having a nap right now."

The mayor took the podium once again. He held up a cell phone and announced to the press: "I have a call here from none other than the governor himself. He'd like to offer his congratulations."

The police chief handed the phone to the twins.

Edgar held it to his ear. After a moment, he said, "Thanks for the kind words, Mr. Governor, but why would we want to support your reelection campaign when we've never even met you?"

Edgar listened to the governor's answer.

"We can have power and influence?" he repeated, turning to his brother.

Allan shook his head no to the governor's offer. "We've had quite enough of ruthless ambition," he observed.

Edgar agreed. He tapped a secret string of numbers into the cell phone keyboard. Surely, a few hundred volts delivered through the earpiece would settle the issue.

The governor's startled scream was audible over the phone line.

Uncle Jack and Aunt Judith groaned.

Edgar handed the phone back to the mayor. "The governor's had his say."

The press shouted more questions. Cameras flashed all around. News trucks beamed the boys' video images across the nation.

Edgar and Allan happily took it all in.

"And there's one more thing," Edgar said into the microphone.

Allan moved beside his brother. "We couldn't have

done any of this without our aunt and uncle, who've not only taken us into their home but also into their hearts."

Uncle Jack beamed. Aunt Judith wiped her eyes.

The boys had surprised themselves. They'd managed to say aloud what they really felt—and in front of witnesses.

⚜ 💀 ⚜

That night, after a celebratory banquet, grateful city officials awarded the triumphant Poe family a two-bedroom suite at the Deluxe Motor Lodge near the edge of town. It had been an exhilarating day, so when Edgar and Allan claimed to be tired and asked to be excused to their room to spend time with Roderick (for whom the motel made a special exception in its no-pets policy), Uncle Jack and Aunt Judith naturally assumed the boys would be asleep before long.

Of course, this wasn't the case.

Instead, the boys sprawled fully dressed for hours on their queen-size beds, neither of which they even bothered to test as trampolines. They were too distracted by questions to jump up and down. So they each just gazed up at the motel ceiling, speculating aloud about Professor

Perry's nefarious but oddly insightful theories regarding their unusual connectedness. No one else had ever quite figured them out so completely.

"So why are we the way we are?" asked Allan.

"Well, in a quantum universe unusual things, like us, happen from time to time," suggested Edgar.

"And that's neither a good thing nor a bad thing."

"Right, it's just an unlikely thing."

"And we're still free to be whatever we choose to be."

"Sure, like everyone else."

"That is, so long as we're always . . ."

The boys stopped, searching for the right word.

"Alike," they pronounced in unison.

Of course the boys benefited from their unusual con-nection. Still, they had to admit that sometimes being two boys with one mind could be a little frustrating. For example, they could never play chess with each other, as each always knew what the other was think-ing. Additionally, they couldn't help wondering if some things, even their least favorite things like health class or gossipy talk shows, might be more interesting if they were able to see them differently from each other, to dis-agree once in a while.

"Of course, it's nice never being alone," Allan observed.

Edgar agreed (naturally), but gave voice to what his brother was also thinking: "Or, being like one boy, are we actually alone even when we're together?"

"You mean, the way your thoughts are also my thoughts?"

"And vice versa."

"Well, there are times . . ." Allan started.

Edgar finished the sentence: "When it'd be great to share our secrets with somebody other than each other, somebody who doesn't already know them."

"Yes, but who?"

Not Uncle Jack and Aunt Judith. And not Stevie "The Hulk" or any of the boys' other classmates, none of whom would ever believe that Edgar and Allan were not just identical but actually interchangeable. It was just too strange. And Edgar and Allan had learned from unnerving recent experience that scientists who *might* understand the connection were not to be trusted.

A chime in the tower of the nearby City Hall marked the hourly passing of the night.

Nine o'clock, ten o'clock, eleven o'clock.

At last, the boys realized there *was* someone they could tell.

At midnight, with Roderick sauntering beside them,

they slipped out of their room, closing the motel door carefully so as not to wake their aunt and uncle in the next room. The night was chilly and the sky clear—perfect for their purposes. They crept through the silent motel parking lot and dashed across the deserted, two-lane highway to where the vast Kansas cornfields began.

Were they looking for more trouble?

No, they were looking for a tiny light in the sky.

It was a snap for the boys to calculate that at this latitude and longitude the satellite launched years before with their unfortunate mother and father accidentally aboard would be visible as a glimmering, orbiting star in the northeast skies from 12:11 to 12:36 a.m. In the almost complete darkness of the cornfields, it would be easy to pick it out among all the ordinary constellations.

"There it is!" Allan observed.

"Mom and Dad, you won't believe all the stuff that happened today," they said in unison to the sky.

And they told their parents the whole story.

"A big studio wants the boys to be in a movie?" Uncle Jack asked Aunt Judith the next morning as the family pulled out of the motel parking lot on their way to the local Pancake House for breakfast.

"Yes," she answered excitedly as she put away her cell phone. "A movie producer just saw the boys on TV and wants them to play the young Edgar Allan Poe in his current project. Isn't that fantastic? Edgar and Allan, movie actors!"

"Not so fast, Aunt Judith," the twins said from the backseat, which they shared with Roderick. They were anxious to get back to Baltimore and to celebrate their overnight fame with their friends—surely the school district would reenroll them now that they were national figures. Then again, being in a movie could be fun. "We'll think it over."

"When do they want the boys to start?" Uncle Jack asked his wife.

"Ten days."

"So soon?" Uncle Jack said.

"They're starting production," she explained.

"In Hollywood?"

She shook her head. "They're shooting the boys' parts in New Orleans."

"Is the pay good?" Jack whispered to her.

"Naturally," she said.

"Well, in that case . . ." he murmured.

Still, the boys weren't certain. There seemed only one place to go for help with their decision.

"How about some Chinese food?" they suggested.

An hour later in a booth at the dimly lit Bamboo Garden, the boys anxiously read their respective fortunes.

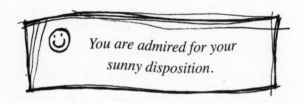

You are admired for your sunny disposition.

And:

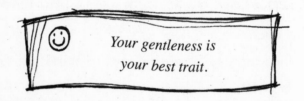

Your gentleness is your best trait.

Astonished, Edgar looked at his brother. "They're *different?*"

"And they're stupid," Allan whispered. "Not even fortunes. Useless."

"They're the same as Uncle Jack and Aunt Judith got," Edgar said, looking over his uncle's shoulder.

"What did you boys get?" Aunt Judith asked.

They crumpled their fortunes into tiny balls and tossed them onto the table. "Nothing helpful."

It seemed they were going to have to make decisions on their own from now on.

"If we do the movie, would there be a part for Roderick Usher?" Allan asked his aunt.

"He could play 'The Black Cat,'" Edgar suggested.

"Good idea," Aunt Judith said, removing her cell phone from her purse. "I'll call the producer and ask him."

"Don't ask him, *tell* him," Edgar said.

"No cat, no Poes," Allan added as Aunt Judith dialed the producer's number.

"The boys have one demand," she said into the phone.

The next day, Uncle Jack drove the Volvo wagon south toward New Orleans along the flat, open road that runs out of Kansas and into the hill country of Oklahoma.

"I hope you two are learning something about geography from all this driving around," Aunt Judith said from the front seat. "After all, there is supposed to be some schooling going on."

"Oh, we're learning about much more than just geography," the boys answered.

"Such as?" Aunt Judith asked.

"Well, we learned it gets hot inside monkey suits," Allan said.

"And we learned it's a good idea to pee every time Uncle Jack stops the car for gas, whether we have to or not."

"No, I'm serious," Aunt Judith protested, ever the professional educator. "Tell me something you two have learned that you didn't know before."

"Hey, peeing is a serious matter when you're in a car for thousands of miles," Allan insisted.

"Yeah," added Edgar, "and it's no small thing to know

that next time we wear monkey suits we'll put ice cubes in our underwear to stay cool."

Exasperated, Aunt Judith put her hands over her face.

"OK, Aunt Judith," Allan said, taking pity on her. "We did learn some new things about quantum entanglement. Is that serious enough for you?"

Aunt Judith perked up, smiling back at the boys.

"I don't understand that quantum stuff," Uncle Jack said.

Neither did the boys—at least, not completely. But that didn't bother them. Actually, little did bother them now that they had a purring Roderick Usher on their laps and the latest books in the True Tales of Horror series (a gift from the mayor) to keep their joined minds occupied.

"Maybe someday we should write our own 'true tale of horror,'" Edgar suggested to his brother.

"Good idea. Except . . . nothing horrible ever happens to us."

"Yeah, it's too bad our lives are so dull," Edgar said.

Allan shrugged. "Maybe we'll get lucky someday."

"Right," Edgar said hopefully. "Maybe something truly horrible lies in wait for us just around the next corner."

WHAT THE POE TWINS DID NOT KNOW . . .

LOCAL NEWSPAPER ARTICLE PUBLISHED TWO DAYS
AFTER THE POE FAMILY'S DEPARTURE FROM KANSAS

Kansas City Post, Crime Section, **PAGE C-1**

CRIMINAL PROFESSOR ESCAPES CUSTODY

CENTERVILLE, Kan. — Centerville Police Chief John J. Stanley confirmed today that Professor S. Pangborn Perry (a.k.a. Professor Marvel), mastermind of the criminal activity recently uncovered at the Gale Farm and OZitorium, has escaped from the Centerville Hospital, where he'd been under observation for a head injury. Police warn citizens that he is to be considered armed and dangerous.

At approximately two p.m., a nurse entered the room and discovered Professor Perry's police guard unconscious on the floor. The guard had been injected with a sedative intended for Professor Perry. Police officials speculate that Professor Perry feigned unconsciousness for an unspecified period of time before attacking his guard. Security video further indicates that Professor Perry, who was believed to be confined to a wheelchair, actually ran out of the hospital, making a speedy escape.

Police have issued an all-points bulletin and request that local residents report any sighting of the escaped felon to authorities.

Mr. Poe in the Great Beyond

Mr. E. A. Poe had been demoted from the Fortune Cookie Division to the License Plate Division. Years of working on fortunes had taught him to get a message across with very few words. He had never fully appreciated the Japanese masters of haiku poetry when he was alive, but writing fortune cookies had opened his eyes. That was one of the good things about being in this place: you had a chance to appreciate new ideas. However, *everyone* agreed that one of the not-so-good things about this place was the License Plate Division.

Being brief is one thing, but trying to communicate secret messages via license plates is almost impossible. Of course, this was precisely why Mr. Poe was moved here by Mr. Shakespeare, who lectured him for what seemed half an eternity about the cosmic dangers associated with secret inter-world messages (even Mr. Poe's successful, life-saving altering of the *Kansas City Post* failed to persuade his boss).

Still, the License Plate Division?

"Isn't that a little harsh, Mr. Shakespeare?" Mr. Poe asked when he was first demoted. "Come on, don't you have any folk down there on Earth to whom you sometimes want to communicate words of advice or warning?"

In response, Mr. Shakespeare smiled, looking very much like the famous engraving of him in the First Folio of 1623. "Of course I do, Mr. Poe. But that's the difference between you and me. You see, I left sufficient words of wisdom during my lifetime to see to such things for all eternity."

If Mr. Poe wasn't already half bald, he would have pulled out tufts of his hair in frustration. But he chose not to give Mr. Shakespeare the satisfaction of seeing him lose his temper. Instead, he shrugged and pretended to appreciate the "new challenge" of the License Plate Division.

What choice did he have?

Still, he wondered how he was ever to get worthwhile communiqués to his great-great-great-great grandnephews.

He knew that now whenever the boys ate Chinese food they received only ordinary fortunes. Surely they must feel abandoned, betrayed. It was very distressing.

But Mr. Poe remained persistent.

His first effort at working with license plates for a secret communication failed because it was too vague for the family to recognize as a sign of his presence in their lives—the fifth Poe. Jack, Judith, Edgar, Allan, and… Great-great-great-great Granduncle Edgar Allan. Instead, when the boys saw the plate on a passing car, they thought it a lighthearted reference to Roderick Usher.

Mr. Poe's second effort was better, and he hoped Edgar and Allan would notice it and realize he'd been with them all along and would continue to be with them, every mile of their journey.

His third try was not nearly as cheery as the first two. Rather, it conveyed his concern over a new nefarious plot that he saw unfolding in the world of his beloved great-great-great-great grandnephews.

ACKNOWLEDGMENTS

My thanks to those who lent a hand to Edgar, Allan, and me:

First, to Kelly Sonnack—my agent, friend, and honorary godmother to the Poe twins—who was always steadfast and encouraging, sharing her quick mind and generous heart to help bring Edgar and Allan to life.

To my editor at Viking, Sharyn November, whose expertise is exceeded only by her adventurous spirit, which resonates in these pages.

To Sam Zuppardi, whose unique vision and wit could charm even the most ghoulish of E. A. Poe's creations.

To Eileen Savage, whose stylish book design brought it all together.

To my friends who read and commented on early drafts, particularly Roy Langsdon, Chris and Don Zappia, and Julie Jones.

Finally, no author has ever been blessed with finer inspirations for a story about smart, enterprising boys than I, thanks to my sons Jonathan, Shane, and Harlan.

And, once again, to Julie, whose love underlies and exceeds all my words. —G. M.

A great big thank you to Jade—will you marry me? —S. Z.

GORDON McALPINE is the author of adult novels ranging from magical realism to hard-boiled literary mystery. This is his first work for younger readers. He lives with his wife in Southern California.

Visit the Poe twins at www.The-poes.net, and Gordon at www.gordonmcalpine.net.

SAM ZUPPARDI used to draw pictures at school when he was supposed to be doing work.

He now lives in York, England—a particularly good city for ghost walks. His picture book *The Nowhere Box* is also out this year. Visit www.samzuppardi.com for more.